T0208842

A Heart of Gold

Un Corazon De Oro

Linda Tomlin

iUniverse, Inc.
New York   Bloomington

A HEART OF GOLD
Un Corazon De Oro

iUniverse books may be ordered through booksellers or by contacting:

iUniverse
1663 Liberty Drive
Bloomington, IN 47403
www.iuniverse.com
1-800-Authors (1-800-288-4677)

Because of the dynamic nature of the Internet, any Web addresses or links contained in this book may have changed since publication and may no longer be valid. The views expressed in this work are solely those of the author and do not necessarily reflect the views of the publisher, and the publisher hereby disclaims any responsibility for them.

ISBN: 978-1-4401-2961-2 (pbk)
ISBN: 978-1-4401-2962-9 (ebk)

Printed in the United States of America

iUniverse rev. date: 3/20/2009

A Heart of Gold

This story begins with a man who is a famous singer. He sings Mexican music, and plays many different instruments. The members of his band dress the same during their concerts. They have their own dance steps to their songs.

His parents are very proud of him. He is very unique, in his own style.

Tomas lives in Mexico, where he has a beautiful home, new car, and owns the bus, which he takes on his tours. The bus is like his second home.

All their schedules are set in advance, so they know where they are suppose to be. His driver is a very good friend of his. He handles everything, including all reservations, and the paper work.

This job is very hard, but he sure loves it. Tomas is a young singer who has been doing this for a while. His voice is so smooth and wonderful, they just love it.

The women love his concerts; once he comes out on stage , they go crazy. After he starts singing, they run to the stage. As the music plays on, they all dance. After he plays the first song, he talks a while. He tells them the announcer is coming out to introduce them to the crowd. Everyone is announced one by one, so everyone knows all about them.

The music plays , and they sing along. (Most of his songs are well-known.) Their hands swing back and forth , while people are dancing.

It is a wonderful sight to see. The action is so awesome. He sure knows how to start the crowds. The women throw roses at him and smile. Tomas loves singing; it doesn't matter to him, because his dance steps are perfect. The concerts last four to five hours long , mostly weekends.

That doesn't leave Tomas a lot of time to do anything. His parents mentioned to him, that they would like for him to meet a nice girl someday, settle down, and, or, get married. They only see him when his concerts are

1

close by. Of course, it's hard to date, or even see someone, because it's too hard to meet them, being on the road.

Tomas explained to his parents, that he doesn't know yet, if he is ready to marry. He says, "There is no woman that I can say, I'm in love with.

"My idea woman would be, one who can cook, especially the Mexican foods, have kids, that's pretty, and that loves only me. She would be the special one to share my life with forever.

"Women that I have met, just want money, things I have or give them. There is more to life that I want.

"If they decide to get mad, leave, then I have nothing. I think it is so important to find the right one. There will be a day, when I'm not looking around, and she will come out of nowhere, she will be the one. Until then, I'm going to sing, and keep looking."

There was a concert in Colorado coming up soon. Everything seemed to be going smooth.

It is set up like any other concert. Things are getting ready, instruments are getting loaded one by one. The luggage is getting packed, and, all the major reservations were set. things were prepared, when it was time .

Tomas is talking to everyone about the concert. Everyone is at the bus talking. He said, "We are almost ready; when the time comes, we should be ready to go."

Everyone was talking, as Tomas walked around the other side of the bus, to check something, he began holding his head. He had a bad headache, but didn't say anything to anyone. Not knowing what was about to happen, Tomas fell.

He tried to get up, but he couldn't. He yelled at his friends. They heard him, all of a sudden, by the time they got there, Tomas felt dizzy, and fell.

One of his friends ran to get a car to take him to the hospital. They wanted to drive him there, they thought it would be alot faster. As his friends picked him up, they got his body into the back seat.

They told everyone to meet them at the hospital. His friends were speaking Spanish to him. They kept saying over, and over, "Tomas, what's wrong? Wake up, Tomas, hey, wake up."

They kept calling his name; it didn't work. His friends were scared. They had no idea what was wrong.

As they arrived at the emergency room, they just jumped out to run and get the doctor. He said to the nurses on duty, "Get things ready, we have an emergency! This patient needs medical attention." "Please get a gurney, call ahead to get things ready, I'm on my way.

"We need to run some tests, we need his family here, and maybe some papers to sign, or to ask questions. Can someone call his family right now? "I need someone here to tell me what happened. I understand a little Spanish, but not everything, I need answers.

"What was he doing before he arrived here? Did he complain of a headache, was he sick before?"

Alot of questions were being asked. Some of his friends were still trying to get a hold of his family.

Tomas was taken to a room where the doctor, and nurses, were working on him.

Lots of people were working that night, things were getting done fast.

One nurse started his I.V., another was drawing blood, it was nice watching them work. All his friends were nervous. Another nurse came and said, "I would like for you all to come with me to this waiting room. I need you to wait here, while the doctor is working, as soon as I know anything, we will tell you more. Please wait."

While they waited, someone suggested a prayer. That was a good idea; they prayed.

About thirty minutes later, a nurse entered. She said, "Has the family arrived yet? "We need someone to translate to them what's going on. The doctor needs more medical information. 'Can you call to see if they are on their way?"

They called the family. Finally reaching them, they were almost there. Within minutes, they arrived. One of Tomas' friends went to meet them to explain everything. They told them about the doctor, and about running lots of tests.

Everyone sat down and waited. They were all talking in Spanish about Tomas. Trying to explain to them what happened, they wondered what made him fall. There was no idea why this happened.

After a while, they got up, and started pacing the floor. It was hard for them to stay still.

About four hours later, the doctor came to visit the family. He explained to them, "Could I please have someone explain in Spanish? I'm not too good with the words, anyway. Tomas is going to have surgery. He has a small tumor that is swollen. His brain has built up pressure inside his head, that's what causing his headaches, it also made him faint. He will be in the hospital for a while. I really don't want any visitors, for a while. Please be calm, I will let you know how everything goes."

The family was scared. They didn't know what to do. Just being there for him, was good. They all sat there and waited.

Finally, hours later, the doctor had returned. Again he asked someone to translate. He said, "Everything seems to be stable right now." We will keep doing more tests as we go, however, we will keep an eye on his condition."

While we are waiting on all the results, you may come in the room to visit, but you must be very quiet." "He is asleep." We are going to keep him at the hospital, to watch him, I need him to get as much rest as possible."

Tomas didn't know he had any visitors in his room, because he was fast asleep.

A few days later, he showed signs of improvement. Everyday, his family and friends came to visit. There was always someone in the room with him. Flowers were brought in from friends, and family.

One day at a time, he seemed to be getting better. As the doctor came that following day, he went to check the charts. He noticed everything was getting better.

One of the nurses went with him, as he walked towards Tomas' room. She asked the family to please translate again, because the doctor wanted to talk to them, He said, "All the tests came out really good. I was hoping for the best, and it looks really good. The report shows the tumor is gone now. Thank GOD. He is showing signs of healing, and he's doing great."

The family was relieved to hear the good, wonderful news. It was so nice to finally hear that everything was turning out well.

Each day, he got better and better. The family decided that they would go down all together to get something to eat. It was a relief to hear the doctor's news. All the family enjoyed their dinner. Most of the conversation was about Tomas. They were excited to visit with him again, very soon.

By the time they were done eating, they were hoping Tomas was awake to talk to them.

Tomas' parents couldn't believe he had fainted. It gave them quite a scare. His mom was talking to everyone, she was saying, "Tomas as doesn't hardly get sick, he did not like going to the doctor's office for his check-ups or anything, I knew it had to be serious when they were saying he went to the hospital."

By the time they all got to Tomas' room, he was awake. Suddenly, he looked around the room. Then he asked his mother, "What happened? Why am I in the hospital? My head, it hurts a little, please tell me what I'm doing here."

About that time a nurse walked into his room. She noticed he was awake, she said, "I'll be right back, I'm going to get the doctor."

When the doctor came in, he asked someone to translate to him in Spanish. He said, "Tell him he's very lucky to have such good friends to bring him here when they did, everything is doing so much better now." We had to do surgery, but all is well. It's a long story, but your friends saved your life. You have a large tumor, the medicine you are taking will make you very sleepy at times. Don't try to get out of bed in a hurry; the nurse will help you. Just call them if you need something. I will check on you again. Just rest and take

4

it easy for now. I'm so glad to see your feeling better and that your family is here with you."

Tomas got thirsty so he decided he did want something to drink. He pushed the button, soon the nurse came to his room and brought him a drink, she asked him how he was doing. She said, "I speak Spanish, I didn't know if you understood me or not, do you need anything else? My name is Teresa. I will be your nurse. Please call me if you need anything. I'm so glad your doing so much better.

"I read your chart I hope you don't mind, I just graduated from my nursing school and they said it's time to go to work so I'm here.

"I am so glad to help people anytime I can. I'm glad to see you smile. You have a very nice family. They have been here everyday since you've been sick.

"I know you need your rest, so I'm going to go see other patients right now but I'll come back to check on your medicines, and everything, anyway, see you after while."

Teresa was a young Spanish girl. She came from a large family. They were raised with alot of respect. She didn't have a boyfriend yet in her life. Her education and school were more important in her life. One of her major goals was to become a registered nurse, and being very determined, she made it, graduating with honors. Teresa was a very nice, sweet person. She knew someday, she was going to meet someone she would fall in love with, also get married someday, when the time is right. Her life is filled with love, loving her job, and working with people.

During her work at the hospital, she was given charts for the patients. As she made her rounds, little did she know Tomas was famous. All she knew about him was written down, showing his condition was improving.

Doing everything she was suppose to at work, Teresa just thought Tomas was a very good patient. She enjoyed helping him.

As she came to work the following day, she noticed family going in Tomas's room. Thinking that he just had a big family, she continued making her rounds. There were people still visiting for quite a while.

When she finished, she went back towards Tomas' room again. As she entered the room, she saw his mom just sitting there. Looking at his chart, she checked about all his medications. Then she turned to his mother and said, "Hello, I'm Teresa, I'm Tomas' nurse, it's nice to meet you. Tomas seems to be doing very well. How's everything doing with you?"

His mother answers Teresa saying, "It's nice to meet you , Tomas is doing well. Everyday, he's getting so much better. Thank you, so much for all your help, we appreciate it very much."

Teresa looked at Tomas, then asked, "How are we doing today? You're looking great. Can I get you anything? I'll be watching for the doctor so I can tell you about any changes. Can I get you a drink? maybe a blanket?"

Tomas told her, "No thanks, I 'm fine for now."

Teresa continued talking to everyone, and smiled. She told his mother she would return shortly. When she left, Tomas was talking to his mother, he told her about Teresa, he was saying, "Teresa is a very good nurse, not to mention she's very pretty. I would like to get to know her more, especially when I'm well. She seems very concerned about me, that's so wonderful how she cares. All of my questions seemed to get answered, she seems to know everything about me, but of course, I'm her patient She's very polite. Do you think she has a boyfriend, what do you think? I'm going to find out more about her if I can."

Tomas and his mother continued talking, soon his friends came to visit. They were glad to hear he was better. It was soon time for everyone's dinner, and he was hungry. That was a good sign for Tomas, that he was hungry.

Teresa brought his food tray within minutes. She came in, putting the tray on his table for him. Everyone began talking again. She asked him, "Do you need anything else?"

Tomas smiled at her then said, "Not at the moment, but I would like to talk to you later, if I could." "Sure," said Teresa.

After Teresa went to pick up all the trays, she went back to Tomas's room. Getting the tray she said, "What can I help you with?"

During this time, Tomas was alone in the room. He thought this would be a good time to talk to her. He said, "I'm so glad you are my nurse, I know this is a big question, but, are you seeing anyone, or are you married?"

"No, I'm not. I just finished school remember, that was my goal. "I wanted that more than anything. Why do you ask?"

Tomas responds, "Well, when I get well, which I am now, would you go out on a date with me? I know you don't really know me, that well, but would you?"

"Sure, I think you're a very nice person, very respectable, and also cute."

Tomas was very happy. She said, "yes," then he smiled.

Teresa got red in the face. She didn't know what to say for the moment, because Tomas' mother had just walked into the room.

Tomas told his mother what just happened. That he just now asked her out, and that she said, "YES." It was so nice that he found someone to make him smile. His mother loved the idea that he had a date when he was getting out of the hospital.

Teresa didn't know about Tomas. She still didn't know that he was very famous. They mostly talked about his condition.

Almost every morning, the doctor would arrive at the hospital early. Teresa told Tomas, "When I see the doctor in the mornings, I will ask him about all your information, and how all your tests came out. I'll have a talk with him, to see what I can find out."

Tomas' family was concerned about him. Teresa would keep them informed. She told Tomas, "It's time for your medication, it will make you a little sleepy, I'll come by later."

Tomas said, "Please come back, I need to tell you something."

As time passed on, about two hours later, one of Tomas' friends came to visit. He was excited to see him. They talked for a while. His friend told him not to worry about anything.

They were supposed to do a concert in Colorado, but it was cancelled until a later time, because of Tomas' medical condition.

More and more friends and family got to visit him, since he was better.

When Teresa made her rounds, she noticed people coming in and out of the room. A few of them left after a while, but one stayed longer to talk. Teresa came into the room. Tomas introduced his friend to her. They shook hands, they talked as the conversation continued.

Teresa heard his friend asking him, "When will you get out of the hospital, so we can set up another concert? Do you feel up to it yet?"

Teresa had a surprised look on her face. She asked him, "What is he talking about? What concert?" She had no clue that he was famous. She just heard what they were saying.

Tomas started talking about the concert again. His friend couldn't believe that Teresa didn't know who he was. Teresa was amazed. All she said was, "What, wait, what?"

All this time she was helping a famous person, and didn't know it.

Later, his friend had left. Tomas told her, "This is what I wanted to tell you. Please stay for a while, I need to explain."

While he was telling her everything, she just sat there in shock. He said, "I didn't want to say anything, because people follow me everywhere I go. They weren't suppose to tell everyone, about my stay here."

Teresa explained, "I did hear something about that around the nurses station, but I thought it was because of your condition. I knew you weren't suppose to have too many visitors, but I didn't know anything else."

Tomas replied, "Reporters always follow me everywhere, I can't go anywhere that they're not there. They were not suppose to know I was here; all they knew about was that I was at a concert."

He explained, "Women call me constantly, they always want to know where I am. As far as they knew, I was out of town, that's all they need to know.'"

Hoping Teresa believed him, he said, "I don't have a girlfriend, I wasn't ready for one right now. People are very interested in my life. I want a normal life, I didn't know I was going to the hospital. "They say there's a reason for everything, guess I'm here to meet someone. you're not like the girls that call me constantly, you're special.

"You came into my life for me to meet you. If I hadn't gotten sick, I wouldn't have met you. You are someone I would like to get to know. Will you still go out with me when I get out?

"Please, I enjoy your daily visits. You're so different, special, sweet, and very nice, will you please?"

"Yes, I will." said Teresa with a smile. "1t doesn't matter what you are, because I think you are special too, I have enjoyed being around you, even if it was at the hospital, these past few months really did mean alot to me. You are a nice person, and I like you, and YES, I will date you."

They gave each other a hug. Teresa smiled, then grabbed his hand. She said, "I have to leave for a while, but I will be back soon, thanks for everything."

Tomas decided to take a nap. It was nice and quiet for a while. He took a long nap, hoping to see Teresa later on.

Teresa's shift was just about over. She was just finishing up the rest of her work. All she could think about was Tomas and what he had said. Everything was a big surprise to her. It was hard for her to believe he was famous. She did realize it, but to let it all soak in at once, was hard. Being surprised that he even wanted to date her, of all the people in the world. She was asked out by a famous guy. She was very happy, though.

A couple hours later, Tomas woke up from his nap. He was already asking about Teresa. The nurses up front told him she was about to finish her shift, so she should be around there somewhere.

When Teresa got there, Tomas asked her to come back soon so they could talk more. He wanted her to stay in his room this time.

When she returned, he asked her, "Do you know when I am going to be released?"

Teresa answered him by saying, "I am not sure yet, but I can find out. I'll see the doctor in the morning. I want to see what he has to say myself. As far as all the reports say, you are doing really great. Now, I can't guess what he might say, but let's wait."

Tomas was glad to hear this. He really did appreciate someone who was concerned. About that time, his family came to visit. They were glad to see Teresa there with him. Everyone stayed a while to visit. After about thirty minutes or so, everyone went to get some coffee. They asked Teresa, "Would you like some coffee, or anything?"

"No, but thank you." said Teresa. "I need to talk to Tomas some more, I want to know more about him, staying here with a most famous person is interesting, a person who has done alot, I just have to find out more from this handsome guy."

They all looked at Tomas. Winking their eye, they were happy for him. After teasing him, they left. Teresa talked to him for a while. She told him she still had things to do so she would come back in the morning. They gave each other a hug, then said goodbye to him and left.

The next morning when Tomas woke up, he was ready to see the doctor. He sat up in his bed, waiting. When the doctor arrived, he went to the nurses' station as usual. He looked at everyone's charts as he did everyday, talking to all the nurses. As he finished reading everything, he was ready to go and make his rounds for the day.

He slowly headed for Tomas's room. Teresa arrived early that day. She wanted to hear what the doctor was going to say. She was excited to hear anything about Tomas, of course.

He came into the room and shook everyone's hand. About that time Tomas' family entered the room. Talk about having perfect timing!

The doctor asked Tomas, "How are you feeling today?" Does your head hurt? Are you having any headaches, or anything?"

Tomas replied, "I feel fine, how did all the tests come out? Does everything look good? When can I get released? What do you say?"

The family translated everything for the doctor. He started laughing, then he said, "Slow down, I know you are ready, but I want you to stay one more day, if you don't mind. If everything's fine, you might get released. How's that sound?"

Everyone was happy to hear this news. Teresa gave him a big hug. She was especially happy for this news." The parents were excited also.

After everyone talked for some time, they left little by little. When all the family left, Teresa stayed longer. Tomas asked her to stay a minute, he wanted to talk. He said, "I need to ask you something. Soon, I will be released. Anyway, I will probably have work, well, a concert to do soon, I'm not sure when, however. I was wondering, when I go, can you go with me?"

Teresa replied, "Well, if you can find out when the date is, and if I can switch with someone, and it's on a good day, where I'm not working overtime, YES. I would love to go. See if you can find out as soon as possible, please let me know."

Tomas told her, "I'll find out as soon as I can, let me get all the information, then I'll know."

Teresa wanted to go, getting very excited, this was going to be her first time. She talked to all her friends at work. There was one nurse that wanted off at a certain time, for her vacation. The timing was perfect, a perfect day off.

"I will work for you, if you trade with me, I really want to go to this concert. Please write it on the schedule if you want, I really appreciate it," Teresa said. Her friend agreed, this was going to work out. It looks like she was going to the concert after all.

As Teresa went to Tomas' room, she entered with a big smile. She told him the good news. All they were waiting on, was to see what dates the concert was planned.

They both talked for a while. The concert was supposed to be real soon, that's why Tomas was hoping to be released in time.

Well, Teresa was tired, then decided to go home. She wanted to change, and get some things done. She told Tomas, "I have to work the late shift tonight, so I need to do some things. Anyway , I want you to rest right now, I will stop by later on tonight, and check on you. I think I will take a nap myself, at least a small one."

Teresa stopped by later, but Tomas was already asleep so she didn't wake him up.

The next morning, she went to see Tomas again. Tomas was hoping to get released, so it was an exciting day for both of them.

As the doctor arrived that day, again talking to the nurses, he looked at everyone's charts again. As he began to make his rounds, he was slowly starting back towards Tomas' room. Teresa had stayed, since she was already there. She told him, she had seen the doctor come in, and he was coming down the halls. Tomas couldn't wait for him to come to his room.

About an hour later, the doctor entered Tomas' room. Asking again, for a translator, he asked how everything was going.

Teresa was already in the room, so she told the doctor she would translate until the family got there. She wanted to hear the news already.

The doctor said, "Well, that's fine, if that's OK with Tomas.

"1'm so glad you're looking so well. Everything on your tests came out really well. If you feel up to it, you can be released today. How does that sound? Just take it easy for now, until you feel stronger, everything should be good."

Tomas said, "Alright, thank you for everything, I really appreciate you, and the hospital for your help. I feel so much better now, I was wondering if someday, you might want to come to one of my concerts? Let me know, I will get you front row tickets."

The doctor laughed, then said, "Thank you, it's good to see you well."

Tomas and the doctor shook hands, thanked Teresa for translating, then said, "I will let you know about the concert."

Teresa and Tomas were happy to hear the good news.

Tomas' family had just arrived at the hospital. Tomas spoke to them in Spanish, saying, "I'm getting released today, the doctor said I was doing fine, and that I'm suppose to take it easy for now, but I'm getting to go home."

Teresa said to them, "1t will probably be a while, because they have to do the paperwork, that takes some time to do."

Tomas replied, "1'm just so happy to leave this place, I will miss my nurse alot though, I loved talking to you everyday, I want to see you everyday, anyway. Remember, we have a special date."

Teresa said, "Yes, I remember, you have my phone number right? I want to talk to you alot more."

After visiting with everyone, Tomas started getting his things ready to go. He was excited about going home.

Some time later the doctor returned. He said, "These are your instructions. Take it easy, drink lots of fluids and don't worry about doing anything in a hurry. They will bring your release papers in a little while. Also you will have to leave by a wheelchair, it's the rules. Good luck with everything, take care of yourself, God bless, and maybe someday I might make it to one of your concerts."

Teresa explained all that the doctor said in Spanish. Of course, Tomas understood a little, but not everything that he said. He knew about leaving the hospital, which made them excited all the rest of the day.

Tomas and Teresa continued talking. She was really going to miss him. They promised to keep in touch.

The release papers finally arrived. Tomas was ready. While all the family came back after their lunch, they heard the news, and were excited for him.

Tomas wanted to talk to Teresa. He said, "If you all don't mind, I have to say something to her alone. It will just be a minute, please."

He said to her, "I'm going to miss you, I really care for you alot, thank you for being my nurse. You are a special person, please call me everyday, I'll be waiting.' Can I kiss you?"

After they starting kissing, the family was knocking at the door. They were saying, "That's enough in there, we can hear your kisses from out here."

Everyone was teasing both of them, when they came out. Teresa blushed.

The time had come to leave.

Teresa walked with friends and family. Tomas was beside her. The elevator door opened, they went in. Going down the main entrance, the doors opened. A car was already waiting outside.

As they got close to the car, Tomas stood up. Everything was getting loaded. He turned facing Teresa, then looked at everyone. He said, "Bye, thank you, I appreciate your help. Teresa, can I have a hug? A kiss too, would be nice, please. Call me when you get off work, I'll be waiting."

Teresa, and his family, watched him get in the car. His friends asked him if he had forgotten anything. As they waited for a while, to get out of the driveway from the hospital, they talked more. Tomas rolled down his window to say goodbye. He was going home.

His friends were going to see him later. Well, it was time to go. Tomas sat back, then looked back at everyone, and waved. He waved until he got all the way out of the parking lot. He was glad to be leaving. It was a very happy day for him.

He was already missing Teresa. They became very close friends. Tomas's friends were glad he was finally getting released.

As they drove Tomas around, one of them wanted just to stop at their house for a minute. He said, "I need you to stop for a minute, I have something I need to do."

Tomas didn't think anything about it. He was just glad to be out of the hospital.

When they arrived at his friend's, he waited for all of them to get out of the car. They looked at him, then he decided to get out.

They all entered the house. As they looked up, they saw a banner, saying, "WELCOME HOME," in Spanish. It was in many colors. Tomas loved it. He shook everyone's hand. As he was thanking them, one of his friends came out of the back room, with his guitar. He began to play a song, soon the others joined him. They practiced for a while. It was like old times. Songs played from the beginning, when they started. Before they realized it, it was an awesome jam session.

One of them played drums on the coffee table, because the drums weren't there. He didn't mind.

They played for a long time. Tomas was playing with the guitar when he came up with an idea. He wanted to play a song for Teresa. He was going to come up with a love song for her.

Slowly but surely, he did come up with a most beautiful song. It was her song. All the band members played along with him. That song was a hit. After practicing, they all had it down. Tomas was so happy being out, he could go back to his life again. He loved playing guitar with all his heart. He loved his friends, as he stood up, then shaking everyone's hand. He loved the welcome home jam session. He then said, "I guess this was suppose to happen to me, because they say, things happen for a reason. I guess you guys are ready to play, have fun, and to start lining up our concerts. What do you say? LETS ROCK!!"

Teresa was sad when Tomas left, but she knew she was going to see him soon. For her, it was time to go back to work. When she finished for the day, she was ready to go home to call him. She couldn't think of anything else but Tomas.

Getting changed, she grabbed her cell phone. Dialing his number, she waited for an answer. He answered it, hoping it was her. They talked for almost an hour. Then he asked her, "I have another call coming through. Will you please hold for a minute?" I'll get right back to you quickly."

Teresa waited. Finally Tomas got back on the line. He told her it was her manager. He asked if he could call her back as soon as they finished talking. She didn't mind. When he did call her back, he said, "It was about a concert, we have one coming up soon, it will be in Mexico. This one was already set up for this date, they were wondering if I was well enough. I need to call my friends, to get things set, it won't be long. I promise I'll call you right back, wait by the phone please."

Tomas got everything arranged. He called Teresa back to tell her about the concert. He said, "I have some exciting news, it's set, are you coming? I found out the date, see if you can go. I know it's soon, but I hope you can go."

The conversation went on for hours. Teresa got more, and more excited. She wanted to call her friend right away to switch schedules. As it happened, her friend said she would switch. Teresa was very happy; it was wonderful. She was hoping it would all work out. Her wish came true.

After talking to her friend, she called Tomas. Waiting for him to answer, she couldn't wait to tell him. She said, "My friend said she would switch. I will get to go. I'm so happy! this is great!! She's changing everything around for work, then it should all work out. Looks like I'm going."

Tomas was happy he was taking Teresa to the concert. He said, "You don't worry about anything, I will take care of all arrangements, I just want you to bring yourself, and luggage, of course. I can't wait!"

The concert was the following weekend. This was going to be the first time for Teresa to see Tomas perform. As the days passed, it was time to get everything ready. Tomas called Teresa and said, "I'll be over soon to pick you up. Are you about ready? As soon as we are done here, I'm coming over."

Within a few minutes, Tomas had arrived. She saw him coming towards the door. Answering the door, she gave him a big hug, and kiss. They talked a while, then he got all her things together. Both of them walked to the car. He set her things down for a minute, opening the trunk, then stopped to open the car door for her to get in. He went back to load the things, getting in the car too, when he finished. He then got another hug.

Tomas talked about helping the guys, and then said, "I love having you with me, by my side. We usually work on getting the instruments ready, then luggage, then relax for awhile."

They talked on the road all the way. It was a fun trip, spending time together. Driving for miles, they decided to stop to get something to eat.

They met the bus at a restaurant. Tomas and Teresa followed them in a separate car so they could talk and relax.

After having lunch, it was time to go so they would make it on time.

Many hours later, they finally arrived. Once they got there, they stretched awhile before going to work. Getting their hotel rooms, finding out where everyone was staying, Tomas and Teresa had their separate rooms.

Things got done fast, all of them helped. After their long drive, they were pretty tired. Everyone went their separate ways, except for Tomas and Teresa. They stayed talking on the bench outside. Teresa still couldn't believe she was there.

It was getting dark. Tomas said, "Do you like sitting by the moonlight? You are beautiful as ever."

"Why, thank you, what a nice thing to say. Yes, I'd love to sit, especially with a handsome guy," said Teresa.

They held each other looking at the moon. As it was getting later into the night, they decided to call it a beautiful evening. It was time to get some rest, so they walked towards their rooms. Tomas walked Teresa to her room. Kissing her on the check, he said to her, "Good night, when you wake up, call my room."

"I'll be waiting for you, I'll get up early. What about breakfast?"

Tomas just laughed, then said, "Can't wait till morning."

The next morning, Tomas knocked. He wanted to see her right away. He wanted to see her, instead of calling.

Teresa was glad to see him too. She kissed him good morning. Then they went out for breakfast.

Now it was time to go to work. Later on that day, was the concert. Tomas and his friends walked over to the bus. A lot of work was being done as they were unloading all the instruments. Everything was being organized, to set up for later.

Teresa helped with the smaller things. She didn't realize how much work there was to do. While everyone was working, his other friend came over to where they were and said, "The coliseum just now opened. They told us to go ahead and get set up. Everything goes on the stage." Then he said, "Tomas, set up the lights, and sound system."

After a few hours of setting up, they took a break. Before they knew it, it was time to eat, then get back and change for the concert. Tomas said, "Now it's time for us to open soon. Would you like to sit up front with us, and family? The show will begin soon. Love you."

Teresa blushed. She was excited for the show. This is the first time to ever see him perform, in concert.

People were starting to show up. The crowds were getting bigger by the minute. She was very amazed how fast it was filling up. As people were coming in, the police came as well. Everyone got their seats, waiting, as the lights staring to dim.

Tomas looked out from the curtain. When he saw Teresa, he waved. He then blew her a kiss.

Everyone was on stage ready to start. Now the time has come.

Slowly, the curtain opened. Playing softly, the announcer came out with his microphone. He was welcoming everyone to the concert. In Spanish, he introduced the band members, one by one. He told the audience, "Hope you enjoy this concert. Thanks for coming, and now the wonderful music plays."

Turning towards them, he waved to start.

The music played loudly. Everyone ran to the front of the stage. Of course, the women went to the front where Tomas was playing. Their hands were up in the air. Some of them were dancing. With all of the music, the band danced. Their songs were all Spanish, so they were doing the moves.

Teresa watched all the people moving around. The place was crazy. She loved it all. Tomas' family told her, it's usually like this.

After a couple hours of playing, another song played slowly, then some confetti was falling down from the ceiling. Everyone acted like they were catching it. It was all different colors. As it fell, the song got faster and faster. Everyone was yelling and screaming. They loved the wonderful music. Some of the people even danced on the sides of the hall. Everyone was having a good time. The band played on. It was wonderful for the crowd. They were having fun.

It was getting close towards the finish. After another song, Tomas waved towards his friends. He looked up, then as they played, lots and lots of balloons came down. The energized crowd got more excited, some of them were dancing the Cumbia dance. That was one of their specialties.

Dancing all around, clapping, having the most wonderful time, the family watched and smiled. As the beat of the drums, to the guitars, the keyboards, the bass guitar, they rocked. Later, smoke came from the stage. People were moving everywhere to the music. You couldn't see them playing, while the smoke was there, but you sure could hear them.

Teresa and all the family, stood up in their chairs. There were so many people, they couldn't see, and they were in the front row. Now and then, Tomas looked at Teresa, and waved. It was dark, except for the strobe lights.

People lit up their lighters in the air, then waved them back and forth, while the music was playing. Loving every minute of it, totally. Everyone was clapping in rhythm, as the music played. Lights were going in all different directions, as certain instruments were being played.

Now it was getting ready for the closure.

The announcer walked on the stage again. He thanked everyone again, for coming. As he was telling them about other concerts coming up soon, in his hands, he had items for sale that would be up front after the concert.

Then he said, "We have something special, that Tomas would like to do before we close for the night. Ladies and gentlemen, Tomas."

Tomas started playing his guitar softly, then said while he was playing, "I have met this wonderful woman, she is here with us today. Her name is Teresa. I would love for you all to meet her. I've fallen in love. Yes, I said in love, with her. Teresa, would you please stand up? I want everyone to meet my special lady."

Teresa stood up; she was blushing. She was happy that Tomas said such wonderful things about her. Tomas played a little more, then he said, "Teresa, this song is for you. This is a love song, I would like to sing for you. You mean so much to me. I 'm so glad we met."

Blowing a kiss with his hand, he began to play. It was a beautiful song.

When it was finished, Teresa went on the stage, and kissed him. The crowd loved it. They all clapped. Tomas gave her a big hug.

All of Tomas's family stood there clapping. Tomas' mom had tears in her eyes. She was so happy that Tomas found someone that made him smile. It was a happy moment for her. It was special to see her son talking about a woman that he loved.

Both Tomas and Teresa turned toward the crowd. He raised their holding hands up in the air. Then they both took a bow.

Then Tomas turned towards his friends. He waved at them to come to the front of the stage. All of them lined up in a row. They took a bow, then waved at the crowd. The curtain was closing slowly, as the concert came to an end.

Everyone was leaving. The family went backstage with everyone. Tomas' mom went to Teresa, then gave her a hug. She was so glad that she came. Loving it, she and Teresa talked while the others were busy.

Putting things away, they loaded all the instruments right away. The work was getting done. After clearing off the stage, sweeping, then locking everything up, they wanted to go get something to eat. They were pretty hungry by then. It was time to enjoy the rest of the evening.

Plenty of conversation was going on at the dinner table. Everyone was talking a lot. Tomas made a toast with his glass of tea. He was saying, "Here's to a wonderful evening with friends, and family. Thanks for everything, I love you all."

He then looked at Teresa and said, "Did you like your song? I made it up, but I thought of you when I was singing, I meant every word of it. It was all true, every word was from my heart. "

Teresa blushed again. She really did love that special song.

After they all enjoyed their meal, they got up, and started back to their hotel. What an exhausting day, or should I say night! They were all tired.

Teresa told Tomas, "1'm very tired, too. Why don't we call it a night, and get some rest?"

"Sounds good to me. Would you mind?" said Tomas, "I am pretty tired."

" Not at all." said Teresa.

"I will call you as soon as I get up in the morning."

They hugged each other, then he kissed her on the check. They both went separate ways.

Not too early the next morning, Tomas called to see if Teresa was awake. She was already awake. Then they were going to meet later for breakfast, before getting ready to leave Mexico.

Everyone was ready to eat by then. All of them went to the restaurant to eat.

About three hours later, it was time to hit the road again. Everything was already loaded, so it saved them some time. All they needed was their luggage.

Tomas and Teresa went to the hotel, to get the rest of their things. Once they got ready, they found everyone else. They were also ready. Tomas followed them in his car. It was time to go.

Tomas and Teresa talked most of the way home. She told him, "I have to go back to work, in a couple of days. I had so much fun, it was awesome spending time with someone like you. Especially, a handsome guy like you. Thank you for inviting me. It was totally awesome."

She gave him a kiss on the check, while he was driving.

The next few days, they spent time talking on the phone. They were on the phone again, when there was another call coming in. Tomas said, "I have another call, let me call you right back, I promise. It's probably the guys."

The band previously had a concert set up before, when Tomas was in the hospital. They cancelled it because he was sick. Now it was rescheduled. After talking with his friend, he told him he was going to call him back later to get more information.

Tomas then called Teresa back. He said, "Hey, remember when I was in the hospital, they want us to do another concert now, guess where?"

"Where?" said Teresa.

"Colorado," said Tomas. "It's beautiful there, speaking of that, can you make arrangements again and go? Can you trade with someone? It's not real soon, but in about three weeks."

"I'll try." said Teresa.

They talked more on the phone. Later on, Teresa called another one of her friends. She talked to her about the schedule at work. It might be possible to trade; they were going to wait until then.

The schedule was pinned up within the next week. Teresa's friend wanted to find her to let her know that her days off, were the days she was wanting off.

Teresa came around the corner, from the hallway, her friend said to her, "Come here, I want to show you something. Remember those days you asked off? Guess what, look at the schedule, girl, it's happening."

Teresa was happy, she called Tomas right away. She told him, "Guess what?" I'm off on that weekend, I want to go again, what do you think? I can't believe it, talk about lucky, I am so excited!"

Tomas was so excited for her. He was hoping she could go again. He told her, "I'm glad you are able to go. I have to get with the guys, to see the plans. I'm not sure what they are doing, but I will let you know right away."

They continued to talk for a while longer. Later that day, his friend called him again. He wanted to make sure all the arrangements were made in advance. It looked like all the plans were finished. All they had to do was to travel when it was time.

As the time passed, it was getting closer to time to go to the concert. Teresa had already made her arrangements so she could go too.

It was getting close to time to get ready. Again, all the instruments had to be loaded on the bus. Everything they needed was loaded as well. Tomas and Teresa wanted to go in his car again, so they could talk by themselves.

Tomas called his family, and Teresa's family. He had a special surprise to share with them after the concert, when everything was over. He told them not to say a word about it to Teresa. All they were suppose to say, was that Tomas really wanted them to go to the concert.

He later told Teresa that all the families were going to be there. He wanted them to enjoy the trip, as well as the concert. He said, "Don't worry, I've already made all the plans, both parents wanted to meet each other anyway, don't worry, we will meet with them when we get there. You will probably see them early in the morning."

Teresa was proud that her parents were coming. She was glad they said yes. She was just nervous about everything. It was all good.

When they finally arrived, they stopped to get something to eat, that was a long drive, but they were very happy to get there.

The concert was scheduled for the next day. Once they relaxed, they went to their hotel to rest. Tomas and Teresa got their rooms next to each other. The band members and everyone found all their separate rooms, they went to sleep for a while.

Later that evening, Tomas called Teresa, he wanted to sit outside of the hotel so they could talk. As it got late, they decided to call it an evening. They kissed, then said good night.

The next morning was a very big day. Both of their parents were going to meet later on. Tomas and Teresa went with the band members to unload all the instruments from the bus. They were setting up the stage for the evening, as the concert was later on. It was going to be an exciting evening, because Tomas already had a big surprise that he was working on for Teresa. Tomorrow he was taking her on a big romantic candlelight dinner, she knew nothing about what was going to happen.

As the time passed, they went to go eat lunch. They knew it was going to be a big day ahead of them, especially, with all the family coming.

Just hours before the time of the concert, both sets of parents and families showed up. Everyone had lots to talk about. Meeting each other for the first time, they were excited to see the concert tonight.

Many different things were happening fast. The meeting room, where they all went to, was full. It had plenty of food for everyone. After things were all cleaned up; and put away, they went to their rooms, to change for the night. It wasn't long before it was time to go to the coliseum where the concert was.

Teresa showed everyone where to sit. People started showing up, crowds of people were coming from all directions. Police and security guards were helping everyone find their seats.

Tomas was excited because one of his long time friends was playing with him tonight. He hadn't seen him in a long time.

Within a few minutes, the curtain opened slowly. Playing softly, the announcer came out on stage. With his microphone in his hand, he welcomed everyone to the concert. In Spanish, he introduced the band members, one by one. He then introduced that there was a special guest playing tonight. One of Tomas' friends was going to play with the band. It was going to be during the half time. He had his own music and dancers, so now let's welcome everyone here tonight. Then he said, "I hope you enjoy this special concert, thanks for coming tonight."

He turned towards the band and waved for them to start. As the music began playing louder, they came towards the stage. Running towards the front, the security guards were watching them all so they wouldn't climb up. It got crazy there for awhile.

Teresa told her family, "1t's usually like this, just wait; you're going to enjoy every minute of it."

The music filled the air, as everyone danced. After about two hours or so of playing, the colorful confetti came down from the ceiling. People were loving it. When they finished the song, Tomas announced that his friend was going to play now.

It was part of this famous concert. He already had dancers on stage. The music was loud and wonderful. Spinning circles, he started the Cumbia dance. He played several instruments. It was very colorful. As he played one of his solos, a girl friend of his joined him. She had a beautiful voice. Behind them were the dancers. It was a great performance.

Tomas again, returned on the stage. His friends joined him. He asked his friend, and everyone to stay and join them. Singing, and dancing, just going back and forth with the music then, Tomas waved at his friend. Alot of balloons came down from the ceiling.

Energizing the crowd, everyone clapped, dancing along. Playing a few more songs, smoke suddenly came up from the stage. You couldn't hardly see them, but you could sure hear them playing. The music was alive, loud, and full of energy.

When the smoke cleared away, the crowd lit up lighters. They moved them back and forth with the music. It was awesome.

Soon, it was getting ready for the closure. As the announcer slowly started walking back on stage, he lifted his microphone, and said, "Thank you all for coming, we have all kinds of items on sale for you after the show. Now we have something special that Tomas would like to do for the night. Ladies, and Gentlemen, Tomas."

The spotlight was on Tomas. He began singing his song. As he got louder, the band played also. His song was the one he had for Teresa. He played it so sweet, and soft. The announcer said, "He made this song for his beautiful girlfriend." When the announcer finished talking, Tomas blew her a kiss. Teresa blushed.

All the people on stage came forward towards the front. They lined up and took a bow. They waved at the crowd. While they waved, the curtain slowly closed. The concert has come to an end.

The band gave each other hand shakes, and high fives, this was a concert to remember. It was an awesome evening for everyone. The families came together when it was all over. As everyone talked, Tomas said to them, "I just want you all to know that we have a special date tomorrow night., Teresa and

I are going on a very special evening dinner. I hope you all don't mind, you can come and meet us later, afterwards, if you want, that would be great."

Everyone teased both of them, but they loved it.

Night time came fast, they were tired, and so they called it an evening. Little did Teresa know what was in store for her the following day.

The morning was calm, everyone started their day. Tomas and his friends were busy putting things up, and cleaning up. Everyone had helped, the day moved on, later, Tomas caught up with Teresa. He said, "I already have arrangements, I hope you don't mind, we need to be there at seven. Can you be ready?"

"Sure, I'd love to." answered Teresa.

It didn't take her long to get ready. She was going to have the evening of her life.

Tomas went to pick up Teresa. She had no idea what was about to happen. As they arrived at the restaurant, the manager saw them coming in. He knew they were going to eat something first. After their meal, and drink, he gave the signal for the mariachi band to go to the table. It was a beautiful evening already, but it was going to be even better. Teresa told Tomas, "We came at the right time. I love their music."

The band played a couple of songs. Then, one of them looked at Tomas, he went to the back of the room. He then, brought out Tomas' guitar. Tomas stood up with the band. They all began playing, of course, it was the song that Tomas played for Teresa.

Teresa was amazed, she smiled, clapping her hands with the music.

After the song, all the customers in the restaurant stood up and clapped also. They loved the song too. Tomas sat down, looking at Teresa, he said, "Are you enjoying your special night? Believe me, there's more I need to do, but first, there's something else I want to say to my sweetheart."

Tomas stood up again, as he reached into his pocket, he pulled out a little box. He proceeded down on one knee, looking at Teresa, he grabbed her hand. His words were, "Teresa, my sweetheart, will you marry me?"

As he looked up at Teresa's face, she smiled, looked at Tomas, and started to cry. She said, "YES, I will!"

Both of them hugged and kissed. Tomas was very happy. That's the answer he hoped for. He got up from his knee, hugged, and kissed her again. Teresa blushed, but she was very happy. She loved him so much, she couldn't say anything else.

Tomas looked over at the mariachi band, they played another song for the beautiful celebration.

Suddenly the waitress came back to the table. She was carrying a cake, and a bouquet of roses. Tomas was so happy, he told the whole restaurant on the microphone, that he asked his sweetheart to marry him, she said, YES!

Everyone stood up and clapped, it was a very happy moment for them.

Tomas told Teresa he would be right back. He had to go do something. He said, "I have to make a quick call, I'm calling the family to tell them the news."

Teresa smiled, and said, "I think you had this planned. I knew you were up to something. That was very nice of you though, because I'm happy too, to marry you. I am very proud, you asked me to be your wife, I Love You Very Much."

Tomas went to make his phone call. When he called everyone to tell them the news, they were excited. He then returned to the table. Teresa asked him, "What did everyone say? Are they coming?"

Tomas told her he talked to them. They were coming.

Before everyone arrived, Tomas said, "I wanted to talk to you, I wanted to ask you this important question, because I had a-feeling you would say, YES. I love you, and I wanted to make sure you felt the same, I wanted to ask you earlier, but I wanted this night to be special. when I first met you, your ways were so beautiful, you are so special.

"You are a very nice person, and your family is very respectful, everything about you is so awesome, my heart and love for you is so great it's like the Lord put us together, he knew we were meant for each other, we'll spend the rest of our lives as one, I am so proud."

Later, after all the families arrived, the manager came over to their table, and put more tables together for the rest of them.

The waitress came over to see if they wanted to order. Everyone ordered food, ate, and then sat there talking. When everyone finished, she removed all the dishes from the table so they could visit. Tomas stoop up and said, "I would like to make a toast, to my future wife, may we have a happy marriage, with lots of kids, I love you Teresa."

Everyone laughed, enjoying the family celebration, very happy that they were going to marry. Tomas waved at the mariachi band to come and play for the table. He put his hand out at Teresa saying, "May I have this dance?"

"Yes, you may, said Teresa.

As the song finished, the family clapped their hands. Both parents of Tomas and Teresa had tears in their eyes. Their children made them so very happy tonight.

Everyone stayed about another hour. Then, it was getting late, they decided to go to their rooms. Tomas and Teresa still had separate rooms.

As the families were walking out of the restaurant door, Tomas stayed behind. He told them he would be there in a minute. He thanked the manager, waitress, and the mariachi band in person for all their work. He was very proud of everything they did for them. He said, "I am so glad my surprise worked, thank all of you very much, I appreciate all your help." He took care of all the expenses, even the good tips.

They all met outside, then went their separate ways. Tomas suggested they go see the band members, after all they wanted everyone to know the good news. Their friends saw them coming, as they got closer to them, they could tell that she said, "YES," by the look on their faces. It was another exciting moment.

"I guess you all already know what I'm going to say, she said, YES, she will marry me. It was such an awesome evening." said Tomas.

They started shaking hands, saying great things, and that they were very happy for them. One band member went to the back room, grabbed the guitars, then the others got out some other instruments. They began playing the marriage song. Everyone played with such joy.

Teresa loved their song. She said, "That was so nice of you all. It was so special, it meant alot to me."

After the excitement, they played a little more just for the fun of it. Tomas then said, "While we are playing, I would like to play the special song for my lady. Will you please join me?"

The band played on, it was great. Teresa sat there looking at Tomas. She loved his music so much, she listened to it as much as she could.

When they all finished, she stood up, shook their hands, and thanked them very much.

Tomas told his friends, "You know I have met the most wonderful woman. I am so glad I have met her, she is a nurse, of course, you knew that, but I wouldn't have met her if I wasn't in the hospital. Just one day, this woman walked into my room, then I saw her face. I knew her face was like her heart. It was like a heart of gold. "She came into my life for a reason, I'm so glad she did." Well, you all know what happened tonight, right?" I asked her to marry me, she said, 'YES', she is so beautiful."

Tomas was a very happy man tonight. He just had to share his feelings with everyone. Later on, they were going to decide on the date, and time, they wanted to marry. Both of them wanted it to be soon. They were excited to plan it.

After making their decisions, the wedding was going to be in two months. Other arrangements still had to be made, but they did decide it was going to be in Mexico, at the church. They wanted it to be blessed, be closer to God, and to be together as one.

Tomas and Teresa wanted a beautiful church wedding. There was alot to do before the big day. As Teresa picked her bridesmaids, she had to decide the beautiful colors they wanted to use in the wedding for all the girls.

When she told the hospital, where she worked, they were all happy for her. The boss told her to take some time off, she deserved it. She was a very hard worker, he was happy to see her get married.

Well, while all these arrangements were going on, Tomas had another concert, before the wedding. It was already booked, so he planned to go before the big day.

He was excited that Teresa was going to be his wife. It seemed like a long time for a special person to come into his life, especially, a person who loved only him. Being single for a long time, was alright, but now he was ready, deep in his heart, to find someone.

Teresa was that special girl. She made him smile, loving him so much, she always wanted a special person to love her too. From the moment she saw him, she liked him. Everything he did, amazed her, being so kind, smiling alot at her, being respectful, but most of all, his ways, seemed to always be polite. Not knowing about him, was better, because she had no idea, he was famous. Whenever she got near him, she was nervous. They met one day, then suddenly, things were changing for them both. It was such a wonderful day, when this did happen. Little did they know, that later on, they were going to be married.

Teresa stayed at this time, knowing all the things she had to do. Her family, and Tomas' family helped her with all the details. They were so excited for the big day.

While Tomas made the arrangements to go to this concert, he had booked, he wanted to do as much planning to help as well. He went ahead and booked a limousine, a honeymoon in Cancun, and the reservations at a very fancy, nice hotel.

All the invitations were sent out ahead of, so everyone could make plans to be there. They were very pretty invitations. The bride and groom's black and white pictures were on it.

The flowers were ordered also. The church was going to have a certain color, while the place where they were taking their pictures, were a little different color. The reception room was going to be decorated with lace, plus white flowers. There was going to be beautiful bells made out of paper on the tables. Hanging from the ceiling, were white paper rolled up and strung all over the area. The arch was going to be decorated with blue and white flowers rolled up all around it. Teresa's bouquet was lots of white roses with satin wrapped around the bouquet. Everything was going to be so beautiful.

Plenty of food was going to be made. Family, and friends were planning the feast. There were about eight or ten tables that had to be decorated to put the food on. It was looking so beautiful. From all kinds of Mexican food, to American, was being made. Two of the tables were the desserts only. You name it, it was there. Very nice, beautiful desserts from cakes to pies, it was great.

Teresa picked out the most beautiful dress. She found it in Mexico, it was decorated with lots of pearls, and lace. The train-veil, was very long. She will need a little help when she walks down the aisle.

It was getting close to the time for the wedding. Everyone was getting nervous already. Tomas had now returned from his last concert. He didn't see Teresa for a few days, because it was almost the day to wed. The wedding cake had arrived, so they contacted the family to find out where the reception was going to take place. It was rolled in carefully. It had four layers of the most beautiful frosting, and it was very big. You could tell it took a long time to finish.

Well, now it was all about to happen. In the early morning hours, the sun came up. Tomas and Teresa knew it was almost time for the ceremony. Both of them were very nervous.

The church began to fill up, people were just coming in, some standing, some sitting down. Tomas and Teresa were in separate rooms. Their families were with them, helping them dress. Both parents were crying, it hadn't even started yet. They hadn't seen each other in a few days, they missed each other.

About an hour later, the priest asked to see if Tomas was ready. He needed to be in the front of the church. Tomas was ready now. As everyone was getting into their places, one of Tomas' friends was singing songs. When his song was finished, a signal was giving, to the rest of the party. One by one, the bridesmaids came with their partners walking forward. The little flower girl came, throwing out rose petals from her little basket. Once the wedding party's family came, and everyone took their places, the priest waved.

The music began to change for the wedding song. All of a sudden, the big, huge, double doors of the church opened, There stood the beautiful bride.

Everyone stood up, then turned around to see her. She slowly walked towards the front of the church. Her father was beside her, holding her arm gently. Everyone had tears in their eyes already. They were so proud, happy, and very nervous.

Upon reaching the front of the church, the priest asked them, "Who gives this bride to be wed?"

Her father said, "I do." Looking at Teresa he said, "I Love You." He turned around to sit with his wife. He was crying silently, but he was very happy.

The beautiful ceremony began. After some words from the priest, he asked them to say their vows to each other. They both looked at each other, then began talking. All of the words they spoke, were sweet. It made everyone cry again.

After the vows, they exchanged rings, lit their marriage candle, and then returned to where they were standing, the priest asked, "Will you please welcome Mr. and Mrs. Velia,"

Of course, it was after he said, "You may kiss the bride."

Everyone was crying as they stood up and clapped. It was a joyful ceremony for them. A perfect love for the perfect couple.

The band members were coming towards the front of the church. Getting their guitars, they began playing a song called, "La Bamba." It was so awesome, watching everyone having a good time.

Their families were all there enjoying the music, talking, laughing, and just visiting each other. The priest came over to where all the families were. He commented on such a beautiful wedding. He was glad to help in any way possible.

Soon, they announced that they wanted to take pictures. Tomas and Teresa took alot of pictures first. They looked so happy. They sure looked nice all dressed up. When the families starting coming in, they were asked to take pictures also. Some of the pictures, were of different sets of families, for all of them to take home. Most of them were of the beautiful couple.

After all the pictures, Tomas said, "I'm hungry, "

Everyone just laughed. They were all ready to go to the reception room, where the food, and the beautiful cake was.

It was customary for the bride and groom, to go through the line first. After them, the priest, parents, and then the families, and friends. Everyone else lined up to get some good food. As they sat down, the priest wanted to bless the food. Everyone was quiet for a minute, as the prayer was said.

Then everyone was talking, it seemed like all at once. There-was such a wonderful feast served. Wonderful music was playing while dinner was served. It was the band, but also friends who just wanted to sing anything. Also, friends sang to the karaoke, or in other words, sing with music playing along with the radio, or record player. Even some of the older folks were singing. Most of them sang the Mexican music.

Tomas played some songs with them. They really enjoyed that. Everyone loved his music.

After the great meal, it was time for the big wedding march. The Bride and Groom, would go under everyone's arm raised up in the air, fingers, touching each other. All of the friends, and families would follow them till the last one finished.

Tomas went on stage again after that. He just wanted everyone to hear the song that he wrote for Teresa, when they first met. He said in Spanish, "I wrote this song for a beautiful woman who I met awhile back. She is a wonderful person. "I want everyone to know, she means everything to me. I love her with all my heart, this is for my wife, here's your song, honey."

When the song was over, everyone clapped. He stood up and took a bow, then walking down the stage, took her hand, and kissed it, then a kiss on the lips.

They hugged for a few minutes. The band began playing more songs. The dancing began again. Teresa asked Tomas to dance. He said, "Sure, anything for you."

Dancing for a while, the families said, "Now it's time for tradition. The men dance with Teresa, pinning money on her dress, for luck. The women dance with Tomas, pinning money on him, for luck. "

This went on for hours, everyone loving every minute of it. Even the smaller children got to dance.

After they all took their turn, Tomas said, "Thank you all so much for everything, you all are so special, we enjoyed everything, we love you all so much."

It was getting late, Tomas and Teresa still had to catch a plane. Both of them walked onto the stage and said, "We have an announcement. It has come time for us to get ready to go, we have to catch a plane, for our honeymoon. Thank you all so very much, for everything, we hope you stay longer, enjoy this wonderful celebration, and again, we love you all so much."

Everyone was teasing them by whistling, and some clapping. They hugged, and kissed their families, on the way to the door. Tomas waved to his friends on the stage, playing songs.

It was time for them to finally be alone. They couldn't wait for the fun to start. After stopping for their suitcases, changing clothes, and the last minute things, they were off to the airport. The limousine picked them up. It went smooth, just like they had hoped. So far, they were making good time.

They were a very happy couple, it was just meant for them to be together. Their honeymoon was for a good three weeks.

It took a lot of planning, for them to get time of together. Sometimes, things happen because it's meant to be.

When they finally returned, they went to see all their families. Teresa went to get her things to move them to her new home. She is living in Mexico now, transferring her nursing in hospitals over there. She decided to work only part time now, because there will be times she wants to go with her husband on tour.

Tomas is still doing tours. He is so happy, it shows in his performance. Especially, when his wife comes with him.

As their lives goes on, Teresa becomes pregnant; she's so happy to become a mother.

Time passes, they have two boys, which are three years apart. As they grow older, they also play the guitar. Their father taught them to play the Mexican music as well. Most of the songs they played, they sang the words as well. When it's possible, they would pack up and go on tour. The others didn't mind at all. They enjoyed the children. Singing with them was fun.

As the story goes, sooner, or later, you will meet someone who loves only you, and that's when you become one in spirit. That's what life is all about.

THE END.

UN CORAZON DE ORO

Esta historia comienza con un hombre que es famoso cantante. El canta canciones mexicanas, y toca diferentes instrumentos. Los miembros de su banda visten iqual durante el concierto. Ellos tienen diferentes pasos para cada danza y cancions.

Sus padres estan orgullosos de el. Es unico con su propio estilo.

Tomas vive en Mexico, tiene una hermosa casa, carro nuevo y es dueño del autobus que lleva los turistas. El autobus es como si fuera su hogar.

Sus horas de trabajo las prepara con tiempo antes para que ellos sepan a donde van a ir. Su chofer es su buen amigo. El hace todo incluyendo las reservaciones y trabajo de papel.

Esta clase de trabajo es muy duro, a el le gusta. Tomas es un joven cantanta ha hecho esto por un largo tiempo a todos les gusta su voz. Dicen que canta suave y hermoso.

A las mujeres les gusta sus conciertos. Cuando sube al foro se vuelven locas el es famoso. Despues de comenzar a cantar ellos suben al foro y la musica sigue mientras ellas estan bailando.

Despues el platica con ellas por un rato les dice que el anunciador viene a introducirlos y los anuncia uno por uno para que conoscan cada uno de ellos.

La musica comienza a hacerlas cantar tambien porque sus canciones son muy conocidas. Bailando y moviendo las manos toda la gente baila donde ellos esten.

Es muy hermoso y fantastico ver y bailar porque el sabe como hacer a la gente disfrutar y a las mujeres les gusta oirlo cantar para ellas le abientan flores y le sonrien.

A Tomas le gusta cantarle a la gente y le gusta bailar cantando lo hace de acuerdo a su musica.

Los conciertos duran cuatro o cinco horas el mayor del tiempo lo hacen en fin de semana y no tiene mucho tiempo para hacer otras cosas.

Sus padres le mencionan que les gustaria que conociera una buena mujer algun dia y que se casara. Ellos lo ven solamente cuando hace sus conciertos cerca porque es dificil tener una relacion y conocer a alguien cuando el viaja mucho.

Tomas les dice a sus padres que todavia no esta listo para casarse porque no se ha enamorado.

Tomas dice,

"Mi idea de la mujer es una que sepa cocinar especialmente comidas mexicanas, que quiera tener hijos y que sea bonita y me quiera solamente a mi. Sera la mujer perfecta para compartir mi vida para siempre."

"Las mujeres que he conocido quieren dinero y las cosas que tengo o les doy. La vida tiene mucho mas cosas que yo quiero y si ellas se enojan se van, entonces me quitan todo. Yo creo que es muy importante encontrar la mujer ideal cuando menos lo espere la voy a encontrar. Ella sera la mujer para mi y hasta que la encuentre seguire cantando y disfrutare mi vida buscandola.

Habra un concierto en Colorado muy pronto todo parece ir bien todo esta quedando listo. Los instrumentos estan llevandose uno por uno el equipaje, reservaciones y todo esta preparado. Tomas les habla del concierto cuando todos estan en el autobus hablando. Tomas dice,

"Casi estamos listos y cuando llegue la hora lo estaremos ."

Todos estaban hablando otra vez. Tomas caminaba hacia el otro lado del autobus para revisar algunas cosas y comenzo a agarrarse la cabeza. Tenia un fuerte dolor de cabeza pero no les dijo nada no sabia lo que estaba a punto de pasar....... Tomas cayo.

El trato de levantarse pero no pudo entonces les grito a sus amigos y ellos lo escucharon cuando llegaron donde el estaba Tomas estaba inconciente.

Uno de sus amigos corrio a su carro para llevarlo al hospital. Ellos lo llevaron pensando que era mas rapido y lo pusieron en el asiento de atras le dijeron a los demas que se encontraran en el hospital.

Sus amigos le hablaban en espanol. Le decian,

"¿Tomas, que pasa? ¿estas mal?" Estaban asustados no tenian idea que estaba pasando con el.

Cuando llegaron al hospital al cuarto de emergencia, le dijeron al doctor lo que habia pasado.

El doctor le dice a la enfermera,

"Tenga listo todo por que es una emergencia el paciente necesita atencion inmediata tenga todo listo por favor en el cuarto de operaciones, necesito hacer unos analizis de inmediato tambien necesitamos a la familia aqui, para firmar papeles y hacerles preguntas por favor alguien encarguese de hacer contacto con su familia de inmediato.

"Necesito alguien aqui para que me diga, ¿Que le paso? Yo entiendo algo de espanol pero no lo suficiente para entender bien lo que le ha pasado a este paciente. Necesito saber, ¿Que estaba haciendo? ¿Tenia algun dolor? ¿Sentia algun malestar? ¿Ha eastado enfermo antes?"

Sus amigos seguian tratando de localizar a la familia. Tomas fue llevado al cuarto de emergencias, donde el doctor y enfermeras lo examinaban ellos trabajaban esa noche para salvarlo rapidamente.

Una enfermera le ponia el suero, otra le sacaba sangre y afuera esperando estaban sus amigos muy nerviosos.

Una enfermera vino hacia los amigos de Tomas y les dijo, "Necesito que todos vengan conmigo al cuarto de espera, necesitan esperar aqui hasta que el doctor venga pero ahorita el doctor necesita tiempo y espacio para trabajar, por favor esperen aqui."

Cuando esperaban alguien sugirio rezar, ¡buena idea! Todos comenzaron a hacer y pedir con sus oraciones.

Treinta minutos despues mas o menos viene la enfermera al cuarto donde los amigos esperan rezando y les pregunta, "¿Ha llegado la familia?" Necesitamos alguien que tradusca lo que esta pasando, el doctor necesita mas informacion medica, ¿puede alguno de ustedes hablarle a la familia?" Haber si ya vienen.

Los amigos de Tomas le hablaron a la familia otra vez. Finalmente los encontraron ya venian en camino y en unos minutos llegaron.

Uno de los amigos de Tomas le dijo lo que habia pasado y les explico todo tambien les dijo que el doctor necesitaba mas informacion medica acerca de la salud de Tomas.

Todos se sentaron a esperar y platicar en espanol, trataban de pensar ¿Por que? Tomas se habia desmayado. Nadie tenia la menor idea, ¿por que? le paso.

Despues de un rato todos estan impacientes dando pasos de aqui para alla, era muy duro estar calmados.

Pasaron cuatro horas luego el doctor viene y dice, "Podria alguien explicarle a la familia de Tomas lo que voy a decir, porque yo no se muy bien el espanol,su familiar Tomas tiene un tumor inflamado en su cerebro. Necesita una operacion inmediata, su cerebro ha puesto mucha presion en su cabeza.

Eso le causo un dolor fuerte y por eso se desmayo. Estara en el hospital por un corto tiempo. Por ahora no tendra ningun visitante, hasta despues de la operacion. Por favor, esperen con paciencia. Ya les informare como procede todo."

La familia de Tomas estaba preocupada sin saberque hacer, tenian miedo por la operacion. Esperar y rezar es todo lo que podian hacer se sentaron y esperaron.

Despues de horas, el doctor viene y le pregunta a uno.de ellos que le tradusca en espanol. Luego les dice,

"Todo va bien por ahora, necesitamos analizar mas pruebas medicas. Mientras, estudiamos los resultados de los analyzis ustedes pueden visitarlo y verlo en su cuarto calladamente Uno por uno sin despertarlo cuando esta dormido."

En unas cuantos dias estubo mejorando.

Todos los dias su familia lo visitaba, tambien sus amigos. Siempre iba alguien y le llevaban flores, cada dia estaba mejor.

Una dia el doctor vino para revizar su progreso de salud.

Todo parece estar bien le dijo a la enfermera,

"Por favor, hablele a una persona para que tradusca lo que le voy a decir a la familia."

El doctor dice,

"Todos los analisis han salido bien, todo indica que el tumor ha desaparecido. Gracias a Dios, esta recuperandose muy bien."

La familia estaba feliz al escuchar las buenas noticias.

Todos los amigos y familia estaban contentos decidieron ir a cenar a un restaurante y platicar felices acerca de la buena noticia. Cuando terminaron de cenar, decidieron volver al hospital para visitar y platicar con Tomas.

Los padres de Tomas todavia no podian creer que Tomas se hubiera puesto tan mal por un desmayo que se asustaron tanto. La madre de Tomas decia,

"Tomas nunca estubo enfermo y no le gustan los doctores ni siquiera ir a la oficina de un doctor para un reviso fisico."

Despues de terminar su cena, todos caminaron por el pasillo, todos platicando iendo hacia el cuarto de Tomas deseando que estuviera despierto.

Tomas desperto' mirando hacia todos lados luego vio a sus padres y amigos y les pregunto,

"¿Que paso? Por que estoy aqui en el hospital? Mi cabeza me duele un poco alguien me puede decir ¿Que paso? ¿por que estoy aqui?"

La enfermera iba entrando al cuarto de Tomas y los vio a todos hablando y les dice,

"Volvere con el doctor, esperen."

El doctor y la enfermera van hacia el cuarto de Tomas. Estoy complacido de verlo ya despierto. Ahi estaba toda la familia. El doctor pregunta,

"¿Hay alguien que tradusca lo que digo en espanol?"

Uno de sus amigos traduce.

"Tomas, usted tiene mucho suerte de tener buenos amigos que lo trajeron de inmediato al hospital. Todo salio bien lo tuve que operar por que tenia un tumor en su cerebro bueno es una larga historia pero sus amigos lo salvaron al traerlo aqui de inmediato. Las medicinas que le prescribo le causaran sueno, no trate de levantarse bruscamente."

"Las enfermeras le ayudaran y descanse es todo por ahora estoy complacido con su recuperacion. Su familia estara con usted."

Tomas tenia sed y queria aqua, apreto el boton para hablarle a la enfermera y pedirle agua. Cuando la enfermera vino con el agua, le pregunto que si como seguia y le dijo que ella habla espanol. "¿Necesita algo mas? Mi nombre es Teresa y yo sere su enfermera de cabecera.

Por favor, llameme si necesita algo mas."

Teresa sigue platicando con el en espanol y le dice,

"Me acabo de graduar como enfermera y comienzo a trabajar aqui. Estoy contenta por que puedo ayudar a sanar personas enfermeras. Veo que sonrie. Usted tiene una familia que lo quiere mucho, han estado aqui cada dia desde que usted se enfermo."

"Bueno usted necesita descansar asi que voy a ver otros pacientes. Volvere despues para darla sus medicinas y asegurarme que este bien lo vere en un rato."

Teresa era una joven que venia de una familia grande que la educaron con mucho respeto.

Ella no tenia novio todavia porque su educacion era mas importante. Su mayor deseo fue convertirse en una enfermera registrada y asi lo hizo y se graduo con honores.

Ella es muy amable y buena persona sabia que algun dia conoceria alguien, se enamoraria y se casaria algun dia cuando ella supiera que era amor verdadero.

Durante el tiempo que Teresa trabajaba en el hospital visitaba a todos los pacientes, leia el informe medico que cada paciente tenia en su respectivo cuarto donde ella se informaba de la condicion de cada paciente y como se iban recuperando diariamente. Ella no sabia que Tomas era un cantante famoso, lo unico que ella sabia era su informe medico.

Teresa hacia su trabajo, ella platicaba con Tomas, le decia que era muy -buen paciente y se sentia muy contenta de poder ayudarlo.

Al dia siguiente Teresa vino a trabajar y cuando iba hacia el cuarto de Tomas vio que la familia de Tomas iba entrando al cuarto de el.

Mientras ella continuaba haciendo sus visitas a sus pacientes, ella pensaba que Tomas tenia una familia muy grande y veia que llegaban mas visitantes al cuarto de Tomas.

Cuando termino de hacer su trabajo volvio al cuarto de Tomas y vio que la madre de Tomas seguia visitando con el, la senoraa sentada platicando. Teresa no dijo nada solo revisaba el reporte medico y todo estada bien.

Teresa le dice a la madre de Tomas,

"Hola, mi nobre es Teresa yo soy la enfermera que se encarga de los medicamentos y la salud de su hijo." La senora le contesta,

"Mucho gusto de conocerla, como esta mi hijo?"

Teresa le responde,

"Todo esta muy bien, el responde muy bien su tratamiento."

La madre le dice,

"Mucho gracias por su ayuda y cuidados a mi hijo, se lo agradecemos infinito."

Luego, Teresa le pregunta a Tomas,

"¿Como la ha pasado hoy? Se ve usted muy mejorado, ¿le puedo traer algo?

Voy a buscar al doctor para darle el reporte de hoy, otra vez le pregunta,

"¿Algo de tomar, una cobija u otra cosa?"

Tomas le dice que se siente muy bien por ahora y muy feliz de estar despierto. Teresa continua platicando con los demas y sonriendo.

Teresa platicaba con la madre de Tomas luego les dice,

"Vuelvo en unos minuntos y se fue:"

Tomas estaba platicando con su madre, le dice,

"Teresa es buena enfermera, muy bonita. Me gustaria conocerla mas cuando ya este yo mejor. Ella parace muy preocupada por mi mejoria es muy alagador verla preocupada por mi salud me cuida y todas mis preguntas me las contesta, ¡sabe todo ¡claro! yo soy su paciente.

Ella es muy atenta conmigo. Verdad que es muy bonita mama? (se rieron.)

Qusiera saber si saldria conmigo, ¿cres que tiene novio? Voy a preguntar un poco mas acerca de ella cuando pueda. ¿Que crees tu?"

Tomas y su madre continuaron hablando por un rato luego sus amigo vinieron a visitarlo. Ellos estaban muy contentos de verlo mejor.

Casi era tiempo para los pacientes de comer su cena, Tomas ya tenia hambre era un buen signo de mejorla.

Teresa trajo la cena para Tomas, cuando iba entrando al cuarto los escucho hablando y puso la cena en la mesita.

Todos seguian platicando. Ella le pregunto a Tomas si necesitaba algo mas ella le dijo,

"Que mas le puedo traer?"

Tomas sonrio luego le dijo,

"Por el momento nada, pero me gustaria hablar con usted despues si usted me lo permite."

"Claro que si," dijo Teresa.

Despues que Teresa recogio todos los utensilios de la cena, ella fue al cuarto de Tomas recogiendo los platillos donde ceno Tomas, ella le dice,

"¿Puedo ayudarlo con algo mas?"

Durante ese tiempo Tomas estaba solo en el cuarto pensando que era buena oportunidad de platicar con ella. El le dice,

"Estoy muy contento con usted como mi enfermera particular. Se que esta pregunta le va a sorprender pero, "¿Esta usted comprometida con alguien o casada?"

Ella responde,

"No estoy ni comprometida ni casada recuerde que acabo de graduarme y esa era mi mayor aspiracion. ¿Porque me lo pregunta?"

Tomas le responde,

"Bueno, cuando yo salga y este mejorado que creoque ya lo estoy ¿Saldria usted conmigo? Yo se que no me conoce personalmente pero. ¿Me aceptar Na una invitacion a salir?"

"Claro que si, yo creo que usted es una persona honesta, respetable, sin mencionar muy bien parecido."

Tomas estaba feliz que ella aceptara su invitacion y sonrio.

Teresa se sonrojo. No sabia que decir en ese momento por que la mama de Tomas entro al cuarto.

Tomas le dijo a su mama que le habia preguntado a Teresa por una cita y que le dijo que "si."

Su mama se siente contenta de que Tomas haya sonreido. Le gusto la idea de que su hijo tuviera una cita en cuanto saliera del hospital.

Teresa no sabia que Tomas era un cantante famoso.

Pues el y ella solo platicaban de su condicion de salud y de su recuperacion cada dia.

En las mananas el doctor venia a visitar sus pacientes. Teresa le decia a Tomas,

"Cuando lo vea le preguntare haber como va recuperando. Le pedire que venga a hablar con usted. "

La familia de Tomas seguia preocupada. Teresa les informaria. Ella le dijo a Tomas,

"Es tiempo que tome su medicina lo hara dormir y volvere despues." Tomas le dijo,

"Por favor vuelva porque tengo que decirle algo. El tiempo pasaba y dos horas despues un amigo de Tomas vino a visitarlo. El estaba contento de verlo hablaron un rato, su amigo le dijo que no se preocupe por nada.

Decidieron cancelar un concierto que estaba planeado hacer en Colorado, se cancelo por la condicion de salud de Tomas hasta que se sintiera mejor.

Mas amigos y familia de Tomas continuaba visitandolo ahora que estaba mejor.

Mientras tanto Teresa seguia haciendo sus visitas a los enfermos, ella notaba que muchas personas entraban y salian del cuarto de Tomas. Unos cuantos de sus amigos se quedaban por largo rato hablando.

Teresa entro al cuarto. Tomas le presento sus amigos a Teresa se dieron la mano y conversaron por un rato.

Teresa escucho a los amigos de Tomas cuando le preguntaron.

"¿Cuando saldria del hospital para poder organizar otro concierto? Cres que puedas?"

Teresa tenia una cara sorprendida ella pregunto a Tomas,

"¿De que esta hablando su amigo? Cual concierto?"

Ella no tenia idea que Tomas era famoso solamente escucho a sus amigos cuando le estaban diciendo.

Tomas comenzo a hablar del concierto otra vez. Sus amigos no podian creer que Teresa no supiera quien era Tomas. Teresa estaba muy sorprendida.

Todo lo que ella pudo decir fue, "¿Que, Que?"

Todo este tiempo ella estaba ayudando a una persona famosa y no sabia.

Despues sus amigos se fueron. Tomas le dijo,

"Eso es lo que quieria decirle por favor quedese un rato necesito explicarle."

Cuando Tomas le contaba todo ella escuchaba anonadada. El le decia,

"No habia dicho nada porque las persona me siguen a todas partes que voy mis amigos y familia no suponian decirle a nadie que yo estoy aqui."

Teresa dijo,

"Yo escuche algo en el cuarto de descanso de todos las enfermas pero yo pense que por su condicion de salud. Yo sabia que no deberia tener muchos visitantes, pero no sabia nada mas."

Tomas le responde,

"Los reporteros siempre me siguen adondequiera no puedo ir casi a ningun lado siempre estan siguiendome. Ellos no deben saber que estoy aqui. Todo lo que ellos saben es que estoy haciendo un concierto."

El continua diciendo,

"Las mujeres me hablan constantemente siempre quieren saber donde estoy. Todo lo que saben es que estoy fuera y es todo lo que deben saber."

Deseando que Teresa le creyera, el le dijo,

"Yo no tengo novia no estaba listo para eso la gente esta muy interesada en mi vida pero yo quiero una vida normal. No sabia que estaria en el hospital y se dicen que todo pasa por alguna razon. Creo que estoy aqui para conocer a alguien y usted no es como las mujeres que me llaman constantemente. Usted es una persona muy especial. Usted llego a mi vida para que yo la conociera y si no me hubiera puesto malo no la hubiera conocido. Es alguien muy especial para mi, alguien a quien me gustaria conocer mejor. Espero que no haya cambiado de idea de salir commigo cuando salga de este hospital. ¡Por favor! yo disfruto sus visitas diarias y usted es diferente, especial, dulce y muy buena. Saldra conmigo, por favor."

"Si saldre con usted, dijo Teresa con una sonrisa. No importa quien es usted porque yo pienso que usted es especial tambien."

Yo he disfrutado estar cerca de usted aunque sea viendolo como paciente aqui en el hospital. En estos cuantos meses usted ha sido especial para mi tambien porque cuando llego al hospital a hacer mi trabajo, tengo el deseo de llegar a su cuarto para hablar y platicar.

Usted tambien es una persona que me agrada y si, saldre con usted.

Se dieron un abrazo.

Teresa sonrio y le tomo la mano. Ella le dijo,

"Tengo que irme pero volvere pronto, gracias por todo. "

Tomas decidio dormir. Todo estaba bien y silencioso por un corto tiempo.

El horario de Teresa estaba por terminar ella terminaba con el trabajo todo lo que ella pensaba acerca de Tomas y lo que el le habia dicho. Todo era una grande sorpresa para ella. Era dificil creer que el era famoso y pensar que queria salir con ella, de tantas personas en el mundo a ella le pidio salir con el estaba muy feliz.

Dos horas despues, Tomas desperto y pregunto por Teresa. Una enfermera del primer piso le dijo que Teresa estaba por terminar su turno que probablemente estaria por ahi en algun cuarto de sus pacientes.

Cuando Teresa paso por ahi, Tomas le pidio que volviera pronto para hablar mas.

Cuando ella regreso al cuarto de Tomas, el le pregunto,

"¿Sabe usted cuando me daran de alta?"

Teresa le contesto,

"No estoy segura todavia, pero puedo averiguarlo vere' al doctor en la manana haber que dice.

Los reportes medicos indican que esta mejorandose. Pero haber que dice el doctor. Yo solo estoy opinando."

Tomas estaba contento de escuchar las buenas nuevas. El realmente apreciaba que ella se preocupara por el. En ese momento su familia llego a visitarlo. Todos estaban contentos de ver a Teresa ahi con el. Todos visitaron por un momento con ella y treinta minutos despues, todos fueron a tomarse un cafe. Invitaron a Teresa, pero ella se nego les dijo,

"Necesito hablar con Tomas algo para saber mas acerca de su persona, estando aqui con una persona tan famosa es interesante, una persona que ha hecho mucho con su vida es admirable. Necesito saber mas acerca the este famoso galan."

Toda la familia de Tomas y amigos miraron a Tomas y le cierran el ojo (bromeando), estaban felices por el. Despues de bromear con el dejaron el cuarto.

Teresa despues de platicar con Tomas le dice que volvera en la manana. Se despidieron con un abrazo luego saliendo le hace un adios con la mano.

A la manana siguiente Tomas desperto listo para ver el doctor, se sento en la cama esperando.

Cuando el doctor llego haciendo sus visitas usuales, hablando con las enfermeras y revisando a los pacientes de cuarto en cuarto.

El doctor casi llega al cuarto de Tomas.

Teresa llego temprano ese dia estaba ansiosa de escuchar el diagnostico del doctor.

El doctor entro al cuarto de Tomas, los saludo al mismo tiempo entro la familia. Perfecto dijo el doctor.

"¿Como se siente?" le pregunto a Tomas.

Le duele la cabeza? Tiene algun dolor?

Tomas le responde,

"Me siento bien. ¿Como salieron los resultados de los examenes que me hizo? ¿Todo esta bien? Cuando me dara de alta? Digame, ¿Que peiensa?"

El doctor sonrio y dijo,

"Momento, momento, se que ya se quiere ir pero quiero que se quede un dia mas. Todo parece estar bien y lo puedo dar de alta que le parece?"

Todos estaban bien felices, las noticias eran buenas. Teresa le dio un abrazo estaba tan feliz por el y sus padres felices tambien.

Despues todos platicaron por un rato, luego se fueron iendo uno por uno. Cuando la familia se fue Teresa se quedo Tomas le pidio que se estuviera un tiempo mas porque queria hablar con ella.

Tomas le dice,

"Necesito preguntarle algo, cuando salga de, aqui probablemente vuelva a trabajar. Bueno tengo un concierto que hacer pronto pero no estoy seguro cuando, de todas maneras quisiera saber si cuando yo vaya. ¿Ira usted conmigo?

Teresa le responde,

"Bueno si usted sabe la fecha y si yo puedo buscar quien me reemplace y si es un buen dia que yo no tenga que trabajar tiempo extra, le dire que si me encantaria ir.

Digame con tiempo cuando sera,"

Tomas le dijo que en cuanto hiciera todos los arreglos se lo hacia saber. Teresa queria ir, estaba muy entusiasmada por ir al concierto seria su primer concierto al que ella iria a verlo.

Teresa les platico a sus amigos en el trabajo y encontro una enfermera que queria cierto tiempo libre, esta era la oportunidad perfecta para cambiar turno con ella. Teresa dijo,

"Yo trabajare por ti si tu trabajas mi turno. "

Yo quiero ir al concierto por favor, si hacemos el cambio de turnos te lo agradecere.

Su amiga acepto estaba perfecto parece que Teresa iria al concierto.

Teresa fue al cuarto de Tomas, entro con una sonrisa le dijo las buenas nuevas. Ya nomas esperaban saber en que fecha seria el concierto.

Ellos hablaron por un rato. El concierto seria pronto en cuanto Tomas fuera dado de alta.

Teresa decidio irse a su casa tenia que hacer algunas cosas y regreso al trabajo por que tenia que hacer trabajo extra. Fue al cuarto de Tomas lo saludo y le dijo que descansara y ella volveria a verlo.

El siguiente dia Tomas esperaba ser dado de alta del hospital y el doctor llego al hospital haciendo sus visitas de rutina.

Teresa fue a decirle a Tomas que el doctor estaba visitando los pacientes. Tomas estaba ansioso esperando al doctor que llegara a su cuarto.

Despues de una hora el doctor entro al cuarto de Tomas saludo y le pregunto como estaba.

Teresa estaba ahi en el cuarto de Tomas ella le dijo,

"Tomas deseaba saber si seria dado de alta e irse a la casa.

Como Teresa hablaba espanol tambien el doctor le dijo que le tradusca lo que dice.

"Estoy muy contento con su restablecimento, todo salio bien en sus test medicos asi que yo lo doy de alta hoy ya puede irse. ¿Que le parece? Cuidese y haga todo despacio hasta que se sienta fuerte todo estara bien."

Tomas dice,

"Que bueno gracias por todo aprecio mucho todo lo que ha hecho por mi usted y el personal del hospital, gracias, me siento mejor. ¿Quisiera saber si algun dia usted vendra a mi concierto? Hagame saber, le dare boletos de primera."

Tomas y el doctor se despiden de manos soriedoel doctor dice,

"Muy bien yo le hare saber cuando voy a su concierto. "

Tomas y Teresa estaban felices por la buena noticia.

La familia de Tomas llego, Teresa les dio la buena noticia todos sonrientes se abrazaban.

Teresa les dijo,

"Probablemente pase un rato por que tienen que hacer todo el papeleaje que tienen que firmar."

Tomas dice,

"Estoy tan feliz de dejar el hospital aunque voy a extrasar mi enfermera particular. Te veo todos los dias que me acostumbre'a nuestras platicas y quiero verte cada dia de ahora en adelante y recuerda que ya tenemos una cita especial."

Teresa le responde,

"Yo se que lo tengo que seguir cuidando y ayudando usted tiene mi numero telefonico."

Despues de recoger sus cosas y visitando con los demas, Tomas esta listo para irse luego el doctor regresa y le dice,

"Estas son sus instrucciones, tome mucho liquido, no haga nada de prisa le daran sus papeles y tiene que salir en una silla de ruedas. Son las reglas del hospital. Buena suerte, cuidese -- mucho y tal vez ire a uno de sus conciertos.

Teresa y Tomas seguian platicando. Ella le dijo que lo iba a extrasar y el le contesta que se seguiran viendo.

Los papeles de salida del hospital llegaron. Al momento llego su familia que estaba feliz porque regresaria a su casa.

Tomas queria hablar con Teresa, les dijo,

"¿Me permiten hablar a solas con Teresa? Unos/minutos por favor. Yo tambien te voy a extranar mucho estoy muy interesado en ti, ya te tengo mucho carino. Gracias, por todos tus cuidados especiales. Por favor, hablame todos los dias, estare esperando tus llamadas. ¿Puedo besarte?"

La familia toco la puerta. Cuando se estaban besando, le decian,

"Ya es suficiente, estamos escuchando sus besos desde aqui."

Todos estaban bromeando con ellos cuando salieron del cuarto. Teresa estaba un poco sonrojada y dijo a llegado la hora de partir.

Tomas se sento en la silla de ruedas que usan para sacar a los pacientes hasta la puerta de salida.

Teresa caminaba con la familia y los amigos de Tomas. La puerta del elevador se abrio' y entraron. Vajan a la entrada principal del hospital. El carro estaba esperando afuera enfrente.

Cuando caminaban hacia el carro, Tomas se detuvo y mientras ponian sus cosas en el carro, el ve a Teresa y a todos y les dice,

"Adios, Gracias por todo, se los agradesco gracias por su ayuda."

Le dice a Teresa,

"¿Me puedes dar un beso y un abrazo? Eso seria muy bonito. Por favor, hablame cuando salgas de tu trabajo, estare esperando porque te voy a extranar."

Teresa y la familia lo vieron subirse al carro. Dentro del carro sus amigos le preguntaban si acaso se le olvido algo.

Mientras iban saliendo del estacionamiento del hospital. Tomas platicaba con sus amigos y les dice adios con su mano levantada desde la ventanilla del carro. Los vere despues, estaba feliz de dejar el hospital.

Los amigos de Tomas estaban contentos de que Tomas estuviera de nuevo con ellos. Aunque ya extranaba a Teresa por que se habia convertido en su inseparable amiga. Pero estaba contento de haber dejado la cama del hospital.

Mientras iban en el carro uno de sus amigos les dijo,

"Detenganse en mi casa por un momento, tengo algo que hacer."

Tomas no dijo nada cuando se detuvieron en la casa de su amigo, esperando dentro del carro con los demas estaba contento.

Despues de unos minuntos, su amigo sale de la casa y les hace senas de que vayan adentro. Todos se miran con curioridad y sin decir nada vajan del carro. Al entrar a la casa ven un letrero colgado de muchos colores que decia,

"Bienvenido, Tomas, estaba escrito en espanol. Tomas estaba feliz y saludaba de mano a todos. Uno de sus amigos trajo una guitarra y comenzo a cantar una canciones luego todos cantaron. Practicaron por un rato canciones de viejos tiempos y canciones nuevas desde que ellos habian comenzado. Poco a poco se fue juntando mucha gente y el sonrio con alegria.

Uno de ellos tocaba tambores en la mesa, porque ahi no tenian tambores. Eso no importaba se estaban divirtiendo, Tomas tocaba la guitarra cuando se le ocurrio la idea de hacer y cantar una cancion de amor para Teresa.

Despacio pero seguro, la fue pensado y cuando la termino era una hermosa cancion de amor para ella. Todos los miembros de su banda lo acompanaron a cantarla y la cancion fue un exito. Despues de practicarla todo estubieron muy felices y contentos de lo bien que salio.

Tomas contento de estar fuera del hospital. Volvio a su vida normal, tocar y cantar con la guitarra y sus amigos. Luego de terminar se levantaba del asiento y saludaba de mano a sus oyentes y admiradores de su banda y musica. Tomas les dice,

"Creo que mi enfermedad paso por algo por ahi dicen, que todo pasa por alguna razon." Creo que todos estamos listos para tocar y alegrarnos la vida, tenemos que arreglar conciertos y fechas. "¿Que dicen? Vamos a mover el bote."

Teresa estaba triste cuando Tomas se fue pero lo veria pronto. Asi que volvio a su trabajo y cuando termino su dia, estaba mas que lista para ir a su casa y llamar a Tomas, estaba ansiosa de hablar con el.

Mientras se quitaba el uniforme ella tomo el telefono para hablarle, el contesto la llamada tan ansioso como ella. Hablaron casi una hora y luego el le pregunta,

"Por favor, ¿Me esperas un momento? Tengo unallamada entrando a mi celular y parece importante."

Teresa espero un momento. Tomas volvio con la llamada de ella y le dice,

"Es el organizador de mis conciertos, Te puedo hablar despues de que hable con el?"

Teresa le responde que la llame en cuarto pueda.

Minutos despues, Tomas le hablo y le dice,

"Arreglamos un concierto que sera pronto en Mexico. Este concierto habia sido postpuesto para cuando yo saliera del hospital. Despues de platicar, Tomas le dice,

"Voy a hablarle a mis companeros para organizar todo. ¿Te hablo despues?" Te prometo que te hablare y espera mi llamada por favor."

Tomas arreglo todo luego le hablo otra vez y le platico lo que habia decidido sobre el concierto. El dice,

"Tengo noticias buenas, ya se hizo el contrato, vendras conmigo ya tengo la fecha y espero que puedes."

Conversaron por horas Teresa estaba muy excitada. Queria hablarle a su amiga, para cambiar turnos de trabajo.

Asi paso, su amiga acepto cambiar el turno con ella. Teresa estaba feliz, parecia que sus deseos se hicieron realidad.

Despues de hablar con su amiga, Teresa le hablo a Tomas y le dijo,

"Mi amiga se queda trabajando por mi, si podre ir estoy tan contenta, ¡Que felicidad!

Tomas estaba muy contento tambien porque llevaria a Teresa con el. Le dice,

"Tu no te preocupes por nada,yo me encargo de todo solo prepara tu equipaje ya estoy con ansia, no quisiera esperar.

El concierto sera la siguiente semana. Esta era la primera vez que Teresa veria a Tomas haciendo su concierto.

Los dias pasaron, ya era tiempo de tener todo listo. Tomas le hablo a Teresa y le dijo,

"Pasare a recogerte, ya estas lista?"

Unos minutos despues, Tomas llego ella lo vio venir hacia la puerta abrio y lo abrazo y beso. Platicaba mientras el recogia su equipaje. Los dos caminaban hacia el carro y el puso las cosas en la cajuela, luego viene hacia la puerta del carro para que ella subiera ya dentro del carro la abraza y besa diciendole,

"Te he extranado mucho. "

Tomas platicando con ella, le dice,

"Me encanta tenerte aqui conmigo cerca de mi. Nosotros usualmente trabajamos en tener los instrumentos listos, luego el equipaje, luego descansamos un rato."

Platicaron durante el viaje contentos de estar pasando el tiempo juntos.

Despues de haber manejado algunos kilometros, decidieron detenerse a comer en un restaurante. Ahi se juntaron a comer con los companeros de Tomas que iban en el autobus, porque Tomas y Teresa iban en su carro solos, para placticar y estar a solas juntos. Despues de comer, era tiempo de continuar con el viaje.

Unas horas mas tarde llegaron se relajaron por un rato antes de ir a confirmar las reservaciones del hotel, donde y en cual cuarto iban a estar, claro que Teresa y Tomas tenian cuartos separados.

Todo se preparo muy rapido para el concierto, todos sus amigos lo hicieron ayudandose todos. Estaban cansados del largo viaje y todos se separaron a hacer sus preparativos. Teresa y Tomas se quedaron platicando en una banca fuera del hotel estaba atardeciendo Tomas le dice,

"¿Te gustaria contemplar la luna? Te vez muy hermosa."

"¡Oh! gracias, " ella le responde.

"Con esas cosas tan bonitas que me dices, si me gustaria contemplar la luna, especialmente con un hombre tan guapo como tu."

Ellos estuvieron juntos contemplando la luna y cuando obscurecio la noche, ellos decidieron retirarse a descansar.

Tomas camina con Teresa hacia el cuarto de ella le da un beso de buenas noches luego le dice,

"Hasta manana, me hablas cuando estes lista para ir a almorzar."

Tomas se rio y le dijo,

"Ahora no puedo esperar hasta que amanesca."

En la manana, Tomas no quiso esperar a que ella le hablara por telefono. El fue a tocarle la puerta queria veria.

Teresa se puso contenta de verlo tambien y lo beso diciendole,

"Buenos dias, "

Luego se fueron para almorzar y llego la hora de trabajar. Tomas y sus amigos caminaron hacia el camion, para preparar todo lo del concierto ese dia.

Todo estaba organizandose Teresa les ayudo con cosas pequenas. No sabia que era bastante trabajo instalar los instrumentos y muchos detalles que tenian que tener listos.

Todos trabajaban y uno de los amigos vino donde Teresa estaba y le dice,

"El coliseo ya esta disponible nos dijeron que nos instalaramos ya." Luego dice,

"Tomas arregla las luces tambien el sistema de sonido."

Despues de unas horas tomaron un descanso y cuando menos pensaron, llego la hora de comer luego fueron a cambiarse de ropa para el concierto. Tomas dijo,

"Llego la hora de comenzar, te gustaria sentarte en frente con nosortros y la familia?"

"El concierto comenzara pronto, te quiero."

Teresa se sentia cohibida pero muy excitada para ver el concierto.

Por primera vez lo va a ver a el haciendo su concierto y la gente comenzaba a llegar mas y mas cada momento. Ella estaba sorprendida de ver como se llenaba el coliseo con tanta gente, tambien los policias llegaron y todos se acomodaban en sus asientos, esperando que las luces se disminuyeran.

Tomas se asomo por la cortina y cuando vio a Teresa, le hizo un saludo desde ahi y le tiro un beso.

Todos estaban en el foro esperando que la cortina se corriera llego el momento.

Despacio la cortina se corrio con musica suave, el anunciador viene con su microfono y les dio la bienvenida al concierto. En espanol, el introduce a los miembros de la banda uno por uno. El le dijo a la audiencia,

"Espero que disfruten este concierto. Gracias por estar aqui y ahora la musica comienza a tocar."

Voltea hacia ellos y les hace una sena de comenzar. La musica comienza muy fuerte muchos corren al frente del foro. Claro que las mujeres fueron hacia donde estaba Tomas y con manos en el aire algunas bailaban.

Con esa musica, la banda bailaba tocando y sus canciones eran en espanol. Asi que bailaban al son de las canciones.

Teresa vio todas los personas moviendose al sonido de la musica, el lugar estaba lleno de gente loca por la musica y canciones mexicanas.

Ella estaba encantada con todo. La familia de Tomas le dijo,

"Siempre es asi."

Despues de dos horas de musica corrida, comenzaron a tocar musica suave luego comenzo a caer confeti en sus cabezas. Todos trataban de agarrar algo de confeti, pues era de diferentes colores y como el confeti caia, la musica iba tocando de despacio a rapido.

Todos gritaban y cantaban, estaban excitados con la musica y otras personas bailaban y la banda seguia tocando. Todos estaban felices y contentos.

Ya estaba llegando el tiempo de terminar despues de otra cancion, Tomas les hizo un saludo a sus amigos. Luego al mirar hacia arriba vio que cantidad de globos caian, mientras seguian tocando y toda la gente ahi estaba excitada con la emocion. Algunos bailaron la danza de cumbia esa era una especialidad de la banda. Bailando y tronando las manos tenian un grandioso tiempo. La familia disfrutaba y sonreia al sonido de los tambores, las guitarras, y todos los instrumentos musicales. Ellos se movian como se usa, " Al son que les tocan."

Luego, humo salia ahi en el foro y la gente seguia bailando al son de la musica. El grupo de la banda no se veia con todo el humo que habia ahi, pero su musica seguia.

Teresa y toda la familia de Tomas tuvieron que parase en las sillas. Habia tanta gente excitada que aun estando en primera fila ya no podian ver.

De vez en cuando Tomas veia a Teresa y le mandaba un saludo desde donde el estaba con gesto amoroso.

De repente se obscurecio, todas las luces apagadas con la excepcion de las luces estroboscopicas. Las persona. prendieron sus encendedores para poder ver y movian las manos al son de la musica.

Las luces de diferentes colores se apagaban, se prendian en diferentes direcciones, segun el instrumento musical que se estaba tocando en el momento y la gente sonaba las manos al ritmo de la musica.

Estaba llegando el momento de terminar el evento. El anunciador camino hacia el escenario les dio las gracias y tambien los invito para otros conciertos que harian proximamente,

Les dijo, que tenian algunas cosas para vender a la salida despues del concierto. Luego les dijo,

"Tenemos algo especial que Tomas hara antes de terminar. Damas y caballeros, Tomas,"

Tomas comenzo a tocar su guitarra suavemente luego dijo mientras tocaba,

"Conozco una mujer muy especial para mi, esta aqui con nosotros-y su nombre es Teresa, me gustaria que la conocieran porque yo estoy enamorado de ella. Teresa, por favor, ponte de pie para que todos conozcan a la mujer que amo."

Teresa se puso de pie y timida pero feliz. Tomas siguio tocando un poco mas luego dijo,

"Teresa esta cancion es para ti es una cancion de amor porque tu eres muy especial para mi y estoy tan contento de haberte conocido."

Le tiro un beso a Teresa desde el escenario, luego comenzo a tocar y cantar su cancion de amor.

Cuando al terminar de cantar Tomas, Teresa subio al escenario y lo beso. El publico les aplaudio y Tomas la abrazo y beso tambien.

Toda la familia de Tomas se puso de pie y aplaudio. La madre de Tomas estaba muy feliz con lagrimas en los ojos de felicidad, su hijo encontro alguien que lo hiciera feliz, fue un momento inolvidable de oir que su hijo estaba tan enamorado.

Tomas y Teresa ven al publico y el toma la mano de ella levantando sus manos juntas hacen una inclinacion hacia el publico.

Luego voltea su cabeza hacia sus amigos de la banda y los invita a que pasen hacia delante en el escenario.

Todos se alinean al frente hacen una genuflexion y levantan las manos unidas en simbolo de despedida. La cortina bajaba despacio y el concierto llego a su final.

Todos se iban la familia subio al escenario tras cortina para felicitarlos y la madre de Tomas fue hacia Teresa y le dio un abrazo. Estaban felices y platicaban, mientras los demas estaban ocupados guardando todos los instrumentos y recogiendo y dejando el local limpio y en orden, decidieron ir a comer algo porque tenian hambre y decidieron comer y disfrutar el resto de la noche y todos conversaron durante la cena.

Tomas hizo un brindis con su vaso de te y lesdijo a todos,

"Brindo por el exito la compania y carino de mi familia y amigos. Gracias por todo, los quiero."

El mira a Teresa y le pregunta,

"Te gusto la cancion que hice para ti? Cada pensamiento, cada palabra me salio del corazon."

Teresa se sentia muy alagada realmente le gusto mucho la cancion.

Cuando terminaron de cenar, se dirigieron al hotel estaban exaustos esa noche, Teresa le dice,

"Yo tambien me siento cansada hasta manana y descansa."

Tomas le responde,

"Es buena idea descansar te buscare en la manana."

Se abrazaron y le dio un beso en la mejilla y se fueron hacia sus cuartos a dormir.

En la manana no muy temprano Tomas habla para saber si Teresa estaba despierta.

Ella estaba despierta y decidieron de encontrarse para ir almorzar antes de su regreso a Mexico.

Todos se encontraron en el restaurante para el almuerso y tres horas despues era tiempo de comenzar el viaje de regreso y todos fueron al hotel por su equipaje.

Tomas y Teresa tambien fueron a recoger sus maletas todos estaban listos, despues de un rato llego el momento y Tomas los seguia en su carro.

Tomas y Teresa platicaron durante todo el camino de regreso al hogar.

Teresa le dice,

"Tengo que regresar a mi trabajo en un par de dias me gusto mucho y me alegro de haber pasado tan buen tiempo con una persona tan especial y bien parecida como tu. Gracias por haberme invitado, Me encanto."

Le dio un beso en la mejilla mientras el seguia manejando kilometros y mas kilometros hasta que llegaron a casa.

Los siguientes dias se la pasaban hablandose por telefono y cuando estaban platicando por telefono otra llamada llego y Tomas le dice,

"Tengo otra llamada, te llamare luego te lo prometo, probablemente son los miembros de la banda."

La banda tenia un concierto arreglado antes de que Tomas estubiera en el hospital. Ellos lo cancelaron cuando Tomas enfermo y ahora se ha arreglado nueva fecha para hacer ese concierto que se cancelo antes. Cuando Tomas hablo con los muchachos por un buen rato, les dijo que les hablaria otro dia para arreglar toda la informacion.

Luego Tomas vuelve a hablarle a Teresa y le dice,

"¿Te acuerdas que cuando estube en el hospital, se cancelo un concierto? Bueno pues ahora quieren que lo hagamos adivina donde?"

"¿Donde?" pregunta Teresa.

"Colorado," le dice Tomas, es un lugar muy hermoso.

"Podrias ir conmigo?"

Puedes conseguir una companera que te reemplace no sera pronto sera mas o menos dentro de tres semanas.

"Tratar", le dice Teresa.

Ellos platicaron un rato por telefono.

Despues, Teresa le habla a su amiga y le pregunta por el horario de trabajo luego le pregunta si podria cambiar con ella su horario pero decidieron esperar.

El horario de trabajo estuvo listo en la siguiente semana y la amiga de Teresa queria decirle que los dias que ella queria libres ella no tenia que trabajar.

Teresa venia por una esquina del pasillo y su amiga le dice,

"Ven aqui quiero ensenarte algo, "¿Recuerdas los dias que quieres libres? Mira el horario esos dias los tienes libres."

Teresa estaba feliz y le hablo a Tomas para contarle. Ella dice,

"¿Que cres? Si puedo ir contigo otra vez porque voy a tener ese fin de semana libre y hablando de suerte estoy muy excitada."

Tomas tambien estaba feliz esperaba que ella pudiera ir con el y dice,

"¡Que bueno! "

Entonces voy hablar con los muchachos para comenzar los planes no se que estan haciendo pero yo te lo dire despues.

Ellos continuaron hablando por un rato al siguiente dia su amigo llamo y queria que todo estuviera listo con anticipacion. Parece que todo esta planeado lo que resta es la salida el dia indicado.

El tiempo paso y todo listo para el concierto llego el dia y todos los instrumentos en el autobus todo el equipaje listo tambien.

Tomas y Teresa irian en el carro para poder conversar solos.

Tomas le hablo a su familia y la familia de Teresa para invitarlos al concierto, el tenia una sorpresa especial para compartir con ellos despues del concierto cuando hubieran terminado de tocar. El les pidio que no le fueran a decir nada a Teresa.

La familia suponia de decir que Tomas realmente queria que todos fueran al concierto.

Tomas le dice a Teresa que las familias estarian ahi, tambien le dice que no se preocupe de nada por que el queria que sus familias se conocieran.

Espero que no te moleste, nos encontraremos con ellos cuando lleguemos. Probablemente los veras en la manana. Teresa estaba contenta porque sus padres aceptaron venir al concierto estaba nerviosa pero todo parecia bien.

Horas despues las familias llegaron a un restaurante a comer algo y descansar del viaje tan largo, pero estaban felices de haber llegado.

Llegaron el viernes de noche y el concierto estaba planeado para el sabado. Descansaron, se fueron al hotel luego cada cual a su cuarto.

Tomas y Teresa tenian cuartos seguidos uno del otro y los miembros de la banda se fueron a sus respectivos cuartos a descansar.

Un poco mas noche, Tomas le habla a Teresa y la invita a sentarse fuera del hotel y platicar. Ellos se encuentran en la puerta hacia fuera del hotel pasan un largo rato platicando y besandose luego se dan las buenos noches y se retiran a dormir.

La manana siguiente era un dia muy grande porque los padres de ellos llegarian pronto.

Tomas y Teresa fueron con los miembros de la banda para ayudarles a descargar los instrumentos del camion. Se iban adelantar a instalar todo para esa noche.

Todo estaba listo e iba a ser una noche muy excitante. Tomas tenia una sorpresa para Teresa al siguiente dia. La iba a llevar a tener una cena romantica, pero ella no lo sabia.

Durante el dia el tiempo pasaba, fueron a comer. Sabian que iba a ser un dia largo especialmente porque toda la familia se iba a juntar.

Unas horas antes del concierto las dos familias llegaron. Todos platicaban y se introducian por primera vez, estaban muy excitados por ver el concierto de la noche.

Muchas cosas diferentes estaban pasando en el cuarto de recepciones donde todos fueron a esperar y platicar, habia comida para todos.

Despues cada uno se fue a sus cuartos a cambiarse para la noche. No paso mucho tiempo para cuando llego' la hora de irse al coliseo donde se llevaria a cabo el concierto.

Teresa les dijo a cada miembro de su familia donde debian sentarse. La gente comenzo a llegar grupos de personas por todos lados. La policia y los guardias ayudaban la gente a encontrar sus asientos.

Tomas estaba muy contento porque un amigo muy querido iba a tocar esa noche con el. Era un viejo amigo que no veia en mucho tiempo.

La cortina del escenario comienza abrirse despaciosamente la musica se toca tambien suavemente y el anunciador salio al frente con su microfono en la mano dando la bienvenida al publico.

En espanol introdujo a cada miembro de la banda, tambien les dice que hay un invitado de honor tocando esa noche, un amigo de Tomas acompanando la banda musical.

El invitado se presentaria despues del intermedio, pues el traia su propia musica y danzantes asi vamos a disfrutar. Luego les dice,

"Gracias por venir a este concierto tan especial."

El voltea y ve a los miembros de la banda y les da la senal de comenzar. Cuando la musica comenzo a tocar resonante y alegre viene hacia delante del escenario.

La gente se acerca demasiado al frente y los guardias de seguridad se encargan de conservar el orden y cuidar que no subieran. La gente estaba muy excitada mientras escuchaban la musica.

Teresa le dice a su familia,

"Asi es usualmente en cada uno de sus conciertos, veran que lo van a disfrutar mucho."

La musica lleno el ambiente y casi todos bailaban. Despues de dos horas cantando y tocando, el confeti caia sobre sus cabezas la gente estaba feliz. Cuando terminaron la cancion, Tomas les anuncio que un especial amigo iba a tocar. Esa era presentacion especial en su concierto.

Las danzantes ya estaban en el escenario. La musica era con mucho sonido y alegria haciendo circulos comenzo la danza de la cumbia. El tocaba diferentes instrumentos y todos estaban muy excitados. Luego toco y canto solo y se fue acercando su novia acompanandolo en la cancion que cantaba. Ella tenia una voz muy armoniosa, atras de ellos bailaban las danzantes y fue una presentacion grandiosa.

Tomas volvio al escenario con su amigo que lo acompano cantando y los danzantes bailando. Luego Tomas hace una inclinacion de saludo hacia su amigo. Cantidad de globos caian sobre ellos excitando mas la gente, todos aplaudian y bailaban al mismo tiempo.

La musica seguia tocaban y cantaban, luego salia humo del escenario no se podian ver los musicos, pero ellos seguian tocando.

La musica fuerte y alegre los llenaba de energia. Cuando el humo desaparecio la gente encendia sus encendedores y los novios de un lado a otro al ritmo de la musica y fue grandioso.

Llego el tiempo de terminar. El anunciador caminaba hacia el escenario tomo el microfono y les dijo,

"Gracias por habernos acompanado, tenemos algunas cosas para vender despues del concierto, ahora tenemos algo especial que Tomas hara esta noche, senoras y senores, Tomas."

Las luces se dirigieron a Tomas. El comenzo cantando su cancion, la banda lo acompano. El tocaba y cantaba la cancion que le compuso a Teresa. Comenzo tocando suave y despacio diciendo,

"Compuse esta cancion para mi hermosa novia," Miro a Teresa y le avento un beso, ella se apena por un segundo pero es feliz.

La banda vino hacia delante del escenario. Se alinearon al frente y uno por uno hizo un saludo respetuoso de adios al publico.

La cortina se fue cerrando poco a poco. El concierto habia terminado y los miembros de la banda tras la cortina se felicitaban y decian,

"Este fue un concierto inalvidable."

Estubo sensacional,las familias se juntaron al final del concierto y mientras hablaban unos a otros, Tomas les dijo,

"Quiero que sepan que tenemos cita manana en la noche. "

Teresa y yo vamos a tener una cena especial, espero que no les maleste. Nos veremos despues.

Cada uno bromeaba con ellos pero lo disfrutaban. La noche llego pronto todos estaban descansando esa noche.

Teresa no sabia que nuevas le tenia el siguiente dia. La manana estaba calmada y todos se levantaban para comenzar el nuevo dia. Tomas y sus amigos se ocuparon de recoger todos los instrumentos y ponerlos en el camion, todos ayudaban y descansaban, platicaban con la familia. Despues Tomas busco a Teresa y le dijo,

"Ya hize la reservacion y sera a las siete podras estar lista para esa hora?"

"¡Claro que si,!' le responde Teresa.

No le tomo mucho tiempo a Teresa en arreglarse. Ya estaba lista para la noche mas importante de su vida.

Tomas llego por Teresa, ella no tenia la menor idea que pasaria esa noche? Llegaron al restaurante y pidieron la cena primero. Al terminar su comida.

Tomas hizo una sena al mariachi de acercarse a su mesa. Era una noche hermosa escuchando las cancions con mariache, Teresa le dice a Tomas,

"Llegamos muy a tiempo me encanta la musica."

Los miembros del mariachi tocaron una cancions mas, luego uno de ellos fue hacia atras y trajo la guitarra de Tomas invitandolo a que cantara con ellos. Comenzaron a tocar la musica de la cancion de Tomas que le compuso a Teresa.

Ella estaba sorprendida y sonreia aplaudiendo al sonido de la musica.

Cuando terminaron la cancion, la gente que estaba en el restaurente se puso de pie aplaudiendo tambien.

`Tomas se sento y mirando a Teresa le dice,

"¿Estas disfrutando esta noche? Pues ay mas todavia."

"Ay algo mas que le quiero decir a la duena de mi corazon."

Tomas se paro un momento y metio la mano en el bolsillo y saco una cajita, luego se pone de rodilla y mirandola a los ojos le tomo la mano y le dice,

"Teresa, mi amor ¿Te quieres casar conmigo?"

Se miraban a los ojos, ella sonriendo y con lagrimas en los ojos, le responde,

"Si, acepto casarme contigo."

Tomas estaba feliz y la abrazaba y besaba esa era la respuesta que el deseaba escuchar. Se pusieron de pie y seguian besandose ella tambien estaba feliz porque lo queria tanto que no podia hablar de la emocion. Tomas le hizo una senal al mariachi para que tocaran y cantaran de nuevo para celebrar el compromiso.

Luego una mesera viene a la mesa de ellos trayendo un pastel y un ramo de rosas. Tomas estaba tan feliz que tomo el microfono y le dice a le gente que esta ahi en el restaurante que su novia habia aceptado casarse con el.

Todos se levantaron y les aplaudieron, era el momento mas feliz de su vida.

Tomas le dijo a Teresa que volveria en un rato. El tenia que hacer algo y le dice,

"Tengo que hacer una llamada a la familia para darles la noticia. "

Teresa sonrie y le dice,

"Yo creo que tu ya tenias todo esto planeado, yo me imaginaba que algo te traias entre manos y todo esto que planeaste es tan hermoso estoy tan feliz de casarme contigo y me siento muy orgullosa de que me hayas escogido para ser tu esposa, te amo, te amo."

Tomas fue hacer su llamada y les dijo a todos la noticia de su compromiso y todos estaban muy excitados. Luego regreso a la mesa y Teresa le pregunto, "¿Que dijeron? ¿Vienen?"

Tomas le responda a su pregunta y le dice que ya vienen.

"Yo quise hablar contigo antes y proponerte matrimonio, sentia que me aceptarias. Yo te amo y por eso te pregunte antes y prepare todo en especial, cuando te conoci te vi tan hermosa, eres muy especial y te amo. Eres muy buena, y tu familia es muy respetable, todo lo tuyo en tu vida es especial para mi, te amo con todo mi corazon parece que dios te puso en mi vida, el sabia que eramos el uno para el otro y que pasaremos el resto de nuestra vida juntos me siento tan orgulloso."

Despues llegaron sus familias y el dueno del restaurante mando poner mesas juntas para todos ellos.

La mesera vino y pregunto si ordenaban algo, pidieron comida y refrescos luego todos comiendo y platicando disfrutaban la noche.

Cuando la mesera recogio los platos y desocupo la mesa, Tomas se puso de pie y dijo,

"Propongo un brindis por mi futura esposa para tener un matrimonio feliz y muchos hijos, te amo Teresa."

Todos estaban felices sonriendo y felicitandolos por su proximo matrimonio.

Tomas le hizo una sena al mariachi que viniera a sus mesas y tocaran y cantaran, luego pone su mano en Teresa diciendo,

"¿Podemos bailar?"

"Si,"- le responde ella.

Cuando la cancion termino la familia aplaudio. Los padres de ellos tenian lagrimas en sus ojos de la emocion que sentian de ver que sus hijos los hacian muy felices con la noticia.

Todos disfrutaron mas o menos una hora mas, se estaba haciendo tarde y decidieron retirarse.

Mientras se dirigian a la salida del restaurante Tomas se queda un momento diciendoles que los alcanzaria en un minuto.

El les dio las gracias al dueno del restaurante y todos sus empleados quiso hacerlo personalmente, tambien le dio las gracias al mariachi,les dice,

"Que esta muy feliz y agradecido con ellos por haberle ayudado con su noche romantica, estoy contento de que mi sorpresa funciono, ¡gracias! muchas gracias, a todos."

Luego pago todos los gastos y las propinas.

Todos se encontraron afuera y se fueron cada cual por su lado.

Tomas sugirio que fueran a ver a los miembros de su banda, despues de todo tambien les queria dar la noticia de su boda. Sus amigos los vieron venir y al verlos tan felices pudieron adivinar que ella le habia dicho que, "si," a su amigo, ese fue otro momento excitante.

"Creo que saben lo que les voy a decir, ella me dijo que si se casa conmigo,fue una noche inolvidable," dijo Tomas.

Todos sus amigos comenzaron a felicitarlos diciendoles que se sentian muy felices por ellos.

Uno de los miembros de la banda fue al cuarto y trajo las guitarras, luego los demaa comenzaron a tocar.sus instrumentos. Cantaron y tocaron canciones y la marcha nupcial estaban todos muy contentos disfrutando.

A Teresa le gusto la cancion y dijo,

"Todos son tan buenos y todo es tan especial que siempre lo recordare."

Despues tocaron un poco mas nomas para divertirse.

Tomas dijo,

"Ya que estamos tocando me gustaria tocar la cancion especial del amor de mi vida por favor acompanenme."

La banda toco y todos estaban felices, Teresa se sento mirando a Tomas, le gustaba tanto su musica y todo de el que nunca se cansaria de escucharla. Cuando todos terminaron ella se puso de pie y les dio las gracias.

Tomas les dice a sus amigos,

"Ustedes saben que he conocido a una gran mujer, estoy muy contento ella es enfermera como ustedes ya lo saben pero no la hubiera conocido si no hubiera ido al hospital. Aquel dia que ella entro a mi cuarto y al ver su cara, yo supe que tenia un corazon de oro. Ella vino a mi vida Por una razon y me siento feliz que ella este conmigo. Bueno ya saben lo que ha pasado esta noche ¿verdad? Le propuse matrimonio y ella acepto y me dijo que si se casaria conmigo, es tan hermosa."

Tomas era un hombre feliz esa noche y tenia que compartir su felicidad con sus amigos.

Despues iban a decidir la fecha y hora de su boda, ellos querian que fuera pronto pero estaban felices planeando todo.

Hicieron la decision de que su boda seria en dos meses, tenian que arreglar otras cosas porque decidieron que se casarian en Mexico, en una iglesia y querian la bendicion de Dios y estar casados para siempre.

Tomas y Teresa querian una boda eclesiastica y habia mucho que hacer.

Teresa escogia entre sus amigas y familia las que serian sus madrinas, tambien tenia que decidir los colores de vestidos que usarian las madrinas el dia de su boda.

Cuando Teresa les dijo en el hospital donde ella trabajaba, que se iba a casar todos la felicitaron. El jefe de personal le dijo que se tomara el tiempo necesario para preparar su boda, porque ella se lo merecia por ser muy buena enfermera. Bueno, pues cuando todos los preparativos, se estaban 1levando.a cabo, Tomas tenia otro concierto antes de su boda. Estaba planeado con anterioridad y seria antes de la fecha de su boda. El estaba tan excitado con los preparativos de su boda con Teresa que el tiempo se le hacia largo para estar juntos los dos para siempre. Especialmente saber que una persona tan especial para el como Teresa, lo iba a amar solo a el. Habiendo estado soltero toda su vida ahora estaba listo para hacer su vida junto a la persona que lo ama y se sentia dichoso de compartir su vida para siempre con ella.

Teresa era la mujer que el habia buscado y esperado encontrar durante toda su vida.

Sonreia pensando que ella lo queria mucho tambien.

Teresa tambien pensaba en el desde el primer momento le gusto. Todo lo que hizo para conquistarla la tenia anonadada siendo tan carinoso, y siempre sonriente con ella tan ga1ante.y respetuoso pero lo mejor de todo demostrandole tanto carino.

No sabia que era famoso cuando ella lo conocio fue mejor para ella porque se enamor de la persona que era el y no por su exito.

Cuando se conocieron poco a poco se fueron conociendo y enamorandose fue hermoso para los dos el haberse conocido. No se imaginaban que un dia se unirian en matrimonio.

Teresa sabia que tenia muchos preparativos que hacer pero su familia y la familia de Tomas le ayudaban con cada detalle y todos estaban esperando el gran dia.

Mientras Tomas hacia los arreglos necesarios para su concierto tambien queria ayudar en todos los planes para su boda. Asi que el hacia lo que podia y tambien hizo reservaciones para una lemosina el dia de su boda, arreglo todo lo necesario para su luna de miel en cancun y reservaciones en un elegante hotel. Todas las invitaciones se mandaron con anticipacion para que los invitados hicieran planes de acompanarlos. Eran unas invitaciones muy bonitas imprintas con los novios de color blanco y negro.

Las flores fueron ordenadas, la iglesia se decoraria con cierto color, el lugar donde se tomarian fotos tendria diferente color. En el cuarto recepcional se decoraria con velo y flores blancas. Pondrian hermosas campanitas hechas de papel sobre las mesas y colgando del techo papel blanco haciendo espirales. El arco se iba a decorar con flores azules y blancas todo alrededor. El bouquet de Teresa seria con muchas rosas blancas con satin alrededor, todo seria muy hermoso.

Planearon hacer mucha comida, la familia y amigos se encargarian del festejo. Tenian ocho o dies mesas para decorarlas, en esas mesas se iba a poner la comida, todo se estaba viendo muy hermoso.

Comida mexicana y americana se estaba preparando. Dos mesas se usarian para postres solamente. Solo hay que imaginarse todo fantastico con toda clase de reposteria Colorida y deliciosa.

Teresa trajo su vestido de Mexico. Un vestido hermoso de satin decorado con mucha perla y encajes. Tambien,el velo de novia era muy largo necesitara ayuda cuando camine dentro de la iglesia hacia el altar.

Estaba llegando el dia de la boda y todos nerviosos arreglaban los ultimos detalles. Tomas regreso de su ultimo concierto y no ha visto a Teresa por algunos dias.

El pastel de la boda llego. Buscaron a la familia para saber donde estaba el cuarto de recepcion para llevarlo muy cuidadosamente. Estaba hecho de cuatro capas con un delicioso y hermoso decorativo era un pastel grande que probablemente les tomo mucho tiempo en hacerlo,

Bueno, ahora todo se va a realizar en las horas de la manana el sol comenzaba a salir. Tomas y Teresa sabian que el tiempo de la ceremonia llegaba y ellos estaban nerviosos.

La iglesia comenzo a llenarse y los invitados llegaban, unos se sentaron y otros parados.

Tomas Y Teresa estaban en cuartos separados, sus familias estaban con cada uno de ellos ayudandoles a vestirse. Sus madres lloraban y aun no comenzaba la ceremonia.

Ellos no se habian visto en algunos dias pero se extranaban.

Una hora despues el sacerdote pregunto si Tomas ya estaba listo porque necesitaba estar en frente del altar. Tomas ya estaba listo y cada uno de los participantes ocupaba su lugar.Uno cantaba y cuando termino la cancion, una senal se dio y una por una de las madrinas caminaban hacia el frente con su acompanante. La nina pequena tirando petalos de rosas. Cuando las familias tomaron su lugar, el sacerdote dio una senal y la musica comenzo con la marcha nupcial. Las puertas se abren y entra la hermosa novia.

Todos se ponen de pie y voltean a verla caminando suavemente hacia el altar. Su padre la guiaba tomando su brazo amorosamente. Algunos tenian .lagrimes en sus ojos ojos de la emocion que les causaba. Todos estaban orgullosos, felices, contentos, y muy nerviosos.

Al llegar al frente del altar el sacerdote les pregunta,

"¿Quien da esta novia para casarse?"

Su papa contesta,

"Yo," luego le dice,

"Te quiero mucho hija."

Fue a sentarse al lado de su esposa con lagrimas en sus ojos pero feliz.

La ceremonia comienza luego de un rato haciendo la misa, el s.acerdote viene hacia los novios y les dice que digan sus promesas uno al otro. Ellos se miraron a los ojos y cada uno pronuncio las palabras que habian preparado.

Despues, intercambiaron los anillos encendieron la vela matrimonial regresaron a su lugar y el socerdote los pronuncia marido y mujer. Luego les pide que miren a la congregacion de todos los presentes y dice,

"Les presento al senor y senora Vela, ahora puede besar a su esposa."

Todos les aplaudieron estaban felices fue una ceremonia muy bonita y ellos estaban llenos de alegria y felicidad un amor eterno para una pareja perfecta.

Los miembros de la banda venian al frente de la iglesia. Todos con sus guitarras comenzaron a tocar y cantar una cancion, "LA BAMBA." Alegria y felicidad tenian todos celebrando.

Todas las familias estaban, todas sus amistades platicando y saludando unos a otros. El sacerdote salio de la iglesia y saludo a todos comentando que habia sido una boda muy hermosa.

Despues de un rato fueron a tomarse fotos. Primero Tomas y Teresa se tomaron algunas fotos juntos, luego ellos con sus respectivas familias todos se veian tan elegantemente vestidos. Se tomaron diferentes fotos juntos y con la familia para guardar recuerdos de la boda inolvidable. Luego de terminar con las fotografias, Tomas dice,

"Tengo hambre. "

Todos fueron al cuarto de recepcion donde estaba la comida y los deliciosos pasteles.

Es tradicion que el novio y la novia comienzen a comer primero.

Despues de los novios los acompanan, el sacerdote, sus padres, y la familia mas allegada. Luego los amigos y amistades, siguen los demas invitados sirviendose al comenzar a comer el sacerdote bendice la comida. Todos callados mientras el sacerdote reza luego todos conversan y pasan el tiempo comiendo y charlando.

Todo era delicioso y mientras una linda musica se tocaba, Luego la banda y algun amigo seguian tocando o cantando diferentes cancions o musica.

Tambien personas mayores cantaban viejas canciones de sus tiempos en espanol.

De vez en cuando Tomas cantaba con ellos y ellos lo disfrutaban.

Despues de comer era tiempo de la tradicional marcha. El novio y la novia pasaban por el conjunto de arcos que formaban de dos en dos tocandose los dedos de las manor con los brazos en alto en lineas de frente con parejas en lados opuestos. Toda la familia sigue a Tomas y Teresa para pasar por debajo del arco formado para ellos.

Despues, Tomas se puso frente a todos y les pide que por favor escuchen la cancion que el le compuso a Teresa cuando la conocio.

Tomas dice,

"Le compuse esta cancion a la hermosa mujer que hoy es mi esposa. Una persona encantadora que me cautivo desde el momento en que la vi. Quiero decirle que, la amo con todo mi corazon, tu cancion mi amor."

Cuando termino de cantar todos le aplaudieron. Tomas les agradecio con una inclinacion y camino hacia donde estaba su esposa, le tomo la mano se la beso, luego se besan y se abrazan por unos minutos.

La banda comenzo a tocar y cantar mas cancions y el baile comenzo.

Teresa .le pregunta a Tomas,

"Bailamos?"

El le responde,

"Claro que si, mi amor."

Despues de un rato de baile, la familia dice, "Es tiempo del baile del billete, el hombre le pone un billete a la novia y uno por uno todos los billetes prendidos al vestido de la novia con un alfiler. Lo mismo se hara con el novio, la dama que baile con el le pondra un billete uno por uno. Buena suerte."

Esto llevo horas todos bailaban con ellos hasta los ninos o ninas, jovenes y viejos todos disfrutaban bailando con ellos.

Al final Tomas les dijo,

"Gracias a todos, todos son muy especiales para nosotros y disfrutamos su compania, Gracias por acompanarmos en este dia tan especial, los apreciamos mucho."

Se estaba haciendo tarde, Tomas y Teresa tenian que irse al aeropuerto y tomar el avion para irse a su luna de miel.

Tomas les dice,

"Nos vamos a nuestra luna de miel, se quedan y sigan disfrutando esta celebracion y de nuevo les damos las gracias a todos."

Todos les aplaudian y decian bromas, se abrazaban y los despedian. Tomas y Teresa abrazaban y besaban a sus familias. Saliendo tomas les hace .un adios con su mano a todos sus amigos que siguieron tocando para la gente que se quedo.

Finalmente estarian solos. Estaban ansiosos para hacer ellos su propia celebracion. Fueron por sus maletas y cambiarse de ropa e irse al aeropuerto.

La limosina los llevo desde ese momento disfrutaban como un sueno.

Estaban felices y juntos para siempre tendrian tres semanas de luna de miel. Todo salio como lo planearon y al fin estaban casados. Su sueno hecho realidad. Asi tenia que ser.

Cuando regresaron de su viaje fueron a visitar a sus familias. Teresa fue a recoger sus cosas para llevarlas a su nuevo hogar. Ellos viven en Mexico ahora.

Transferir sus papeles para seguir trabajando como enfermera en un hospital de Mexico. Ella decidio trabajar tiempo medio para poder acompanar a su esposo en sus jiras artisticas.

Tomas sigue haciendo sus conciertos y transmite su felicidad en sus canciones especialmente cuando ella lo acompana .

El tiempo ha pasado y Teresa espera un bebe, ella esta feliz de llegar a ser madre.

El tiempo sigui pasando y ya tienen dos ninos uno de seis anos y otro de tres. Los ninos han crecido tocando y cantando en espanol porque su papa, Tomas, les ha ensezado.

Cuando es posible todos empacan sus maletas y van a los conciertos de el.

Los miembros de la banda disfrututan cuando van los ninos y tambien ellos los ensenaron a, cantar y tocar.

Como la historia dice, tarde o temprano, se conoce alguien que sabe querer o amar a la otra persona hasta que se convierten en un solo espiritu, eso es parte de la vida, "Y UN CO'RAZON DE ORO."

Her name is LINDA TOMLIN, and she believes she has creativity in her writting. She loves writing poetry, with two story books, and children's stories. She was in the book of The Best Poets and Poems of 2007. Her poem was called, "A PARENTS LOVE." Linda has also received Editor's Choice Award for 2007.

Some of her poetry has been published with The International Library of Poetry. They are in Owings Mills, MD. Her first book was published with 1st Books Library in Bloomington, ID. She has four children, married 30 years, is a Breast Cancer Survivor. Her books talk about Inspiration, Love, Life, and Poetry.